OFFICIALLY
WITHDRAWN

The
AMBROSE
Deception

2021 Bluestem Nominee

The AMBROSE Deception

by Emily Ecton

with illustrations by Gilbert Ford

Los Angeles   New York

Text copyright © 2018 by Emily Ecton
Illustrations copyright © 2018 by Gilbert Ford

All rights reserved. Published by Disney • Hyperion, an imprint of Disney Book Group. No part of this book may be reproduced or transmitted in any form or by any means, electronic or mechanical, including photocopying, recording, or by any information storage and retrieval system, without written permission from the publisher. For information address Disney • Hyperion, 125 West End Avenue, New York, New York 10023.

First Hardcover Edition, February 2018
First Paperback Edition, February 2019
5 7 9 10 8 6
FAC-025438-20072
Printed in the United States of America

This book is set in Alwyn New, Ambassador Script Pro, Andy Pro, Artegra Sans, Cherily Blussom, Deanna Script, Emily Austin, Fratello Nick, Jelena Handwriting, Lucida Calligraphy, Lucky Fellas Upright, Marydale Bold, Nue, Ondise, P22 Cezanne, P22 Rodin, Qiber/Fontspring; Andale Mono, Avenir Next Condensed, Bell MT, Caecilia LT Pro, Cochin LT Pro, Conduit ITC Pro, Devanagari MT, DIN Next LT Pro, Feltpen Pro, Grimshaw Hand ITC Std, Minister Std, Sabon MT Pro, Times New Roman PS, Wiesbaden Swing LT Std/Monotype

Designed by Michelle Gengaro-Kokmen
The interior art in this book was created using brush and ink.
The cover was created using mixed media digital.

Library of Congress Cataloging-in-Publication Control Number
for Hardcover Edition: 2016038102

ISBN 978-1-4847-9005-2

Visit www.DisneyBooks.com

SUSTAINABLE
FORESTRY
INITIATIVE
Certified Chain of Custody
Promoting Sustainable Forestry
www.sfiprogram.org
SFI-01054
The SFI label applies to the text stock

To the city of Chicago (and its penguins)

At Morton Middle School

The transaction took less than a minute. The red-haired girl slid the completed worksheet across the table just as the boy in the Blackhawks shirt walked by. She didn't look up. And the boy didn't even pause as he slid the worksheet into his notebook, dropping a wrinkled five-dollar bill onto the table in its place.

The girl palmed the five without taking her eyes off of her book.

Neither one of them noticed the two men watching from the corner of the library. They didn't notice as the stocky man gave a subtle nod. They didn't notice the taller man snap a photo.

At Noyes Central

The kid with the bouncy step paused as he turned the corner into the hallway. A large bully was in the process of trying to stuff a small, podgy boy into an even smaller locker, with limited success. Neither the stuffer nor the stuffee noticed the new arrival. They also didn't notice two men watching from the shadow of a doorway.

After only a moment of hesitation, the bouncy kid continued on his way, whistling loudly, seemingly oblivious to the scene at the locker. He was also seemingly oblivious to the bully's books balanced on the trash can.

The bully paused in his stuffing as the kid got closer. "Not your problem, Johnson."

The kid nodded amiably. "'Course not. Wouldn't dream of interrupting." He smiled. "But you do realize you have an audience."

He nodded toward the men in the doorway.

"Wha?" The bully loosened his grip as he turned awkwardly to peer over his shoulder, giving the small, podgy victim the chance he needed to wrench free and make his escape.

"Aw. Tough break," Johnson said, making a sad face before slapping the bully on the back and walking on, pausing only to casually hip-check the trash can as he passed by. The bully's schoolbooks teetered precariously and then fell with a squishy thud into an unappetizing mass of discarded food containers.

The stocky man in the shadows smiled to himself and nodded discreetly. The tall man with him snapped a picture just as the kid bounced off down the hallway.

At Sutherland Academy

In the school office, the secretary rushed forward to greet her two visitors. She stepped carefully over the feet of the sniffly boy seated by the door. His legs, which seemed too long for his body, spilled awkwardly into the traffic area of the room.

She used both hands to shake the hand of the stocky man. "We're so honored to have you with us today, sir. Both of you sirs," she added, smiling enthusiastically at the tall man.

"Not at all," said the stocky man. He wasn't looking at her. He was watching as the sniffly boy cracked his knuckles and then blew a piece of hair out of his eyes.

The school secretary frowned and scanned the paperwork on her clipboard. "Now . . . I think you're all set. You should have everything you— Oh! I forgot to give you your badges." She stepped back over the boy's feet and leaned across the front counter, knocking a pad of tardy slips onto the floor. Without a word, and hardly seeming to move, the boy stretched out a long arm and pocketed them.

The stocky man cleared his throat and raised an eyebrow at the tall man behind him. The tall man discreetly snapped a picture.

"Here you are!" The school secretary proudly held out two name badges. The stocky man smiled at her and shook his head. "That won't be necessary, madam," he said. "In fact, I don't think a tour will be necessary, after all. We have everything we need."

Letter to the Principals of Morton Middle School, Noyes Central, and Sutherland Academy in Chicago:

CONGRATULATIONS!

Your school has been selected for a great honor. Three students have been chosen citywide to compete for a prestigious Kaplin/Baron $10,000 academic scholarship. This is a once-in-a-lifetime opportunity, with very selective screening procedures. The Kaplin/Baron academic scholarship is a grant of nationwide renown, and the schools that successful competitors attend are given additional points toward national rankings.

You will be pleased to learn that one of your students has been selected for this rare scholarship opportunity.

Please contact us at the number listed below to arrange an organizational meeting. This offer will not be repeated.

At Morton Middle School

Morton Middle School guidance counselor Judy Orlin tapped her fingertips on her desk as she stared at the computer monitor. Something was just not right.

"Melissa Burris," she said out loud. Then she frowned as if the name had left a bad taste in her mouth. She typed on her keyboard and sniffed.

"Melissa Burris," she repeated.

"What?" Miss Baker stuck her head out of the copy room. "Did you say something?"

Judy Orlin shook her head. "Melissa Burris. Does that name mean anything to you?"

Miss Baker stared at the ceiling while she thought. Judy Orlin tapped impatiently.

"No," Miss Baker said finally. "Should it?"

"No, it absolutely shouldn't," Judy Orlin said, frowning at her computer again. "She's not one of my Shining

Star gifted students, she's not in any of the Racing Rocket athletic programs, she's not in Mathletes or BandTastic or Chess-perts or the Jazzercise Singers or even the AV club. She's not in anything. She's a complete nobody."

"So?" Miss Baker had fifty copies to make before the bell rang. "What's the problem?"

"The problem, Miss Baker, is that Melissa Burris has been chosen to compete for a prestigious scholarship. A *very* prestigious, once-in-a-lifetime opportunity. And she was the *only* Morton Middle School student chosen. The only one in our entire district."

"Well, that's strange." Miss Baker looked puzzled. "Why?"

Judy Orlin narrowed her eyes and leaned back in her chair. "Exactly."

At Sutherland Academy

Office receptionist Chad Brown chuckled and crumpled up the piece of paper he'd been reading. Then he tossed the wad at the trash can. It landed two feet short, almost hitting three other balls of paper. It bounced sadly and then rolled over to where Mr. Andrews was coming out of the mail cubby.

Mr. Andrews picked up the wad and uncrumpled it. "What's this?"

"Some scam. Scholarship con or something." Chad rolled his eyes. "How dumb do they think we are?"

Mr. Andrews scanned the paper. "Scholarship, huh?" He shrugged. "It's good to be cautious, Chad, but I have to say, this looks legit."

Chad hopped to his feet. "No, I know what you mean—I thought so, too, at first. But see there?" He pointed to the paragraph at the bottom of the page. "They chose Wilf. Wilf

Samson? They didn't even pick a believable kid."

Mr. Andrews frowned. Wilf was in his third-period math class. Most of the time, anyway. "Okay, Wilf. Why not Wilf?"

"Well, you know . . ."

Mr. Andrews didn't say anything—he just waited.

Chad coughed awkwardly and peered at the letter. "Okay, I guess it *could* be real. I just thought Wilf . . . funny kid to pick, don't you think? He's not exactly a go-getter." He'd dismissed hundreds of letters as scams. He didn't see why this one should be any different. But he wasn't going to let a stupid letter get him in hot water, not if Mr. Andrews wanted to believe it.

Mr. Andrews waggled his eyebrows. "Might as well tell him. Not that he'll bother doing anything about it." He grinned as he picked up his coffee cup.

Chad grinned back. What harm could it do? It was Wilf, after all. He probably wouldn't even read the letter. "Sure thing. I'll let him know."

At Noyes Central

It's not that I have anything against Bondi," Mrs. Gray said, pursing her lips as she passed the letter to Principal Bart Fleming. "God knows, he's entertaining enough. But . . . an academic scholarship? Honestly, I can think of a hundred kids more qualified than Bondi Johnson."

Principal Fleming frowned at the letter. "Wait, our Bondi? Really?" He read the later carefully. "Bondi of the lunchroom serenade?" He looked to Mrs. Gray for confirmation. "The one who got that, oh, what was it—?"

"The one who got Sneezy, the classroom rat, elected school president? Who petitioned the governor to make 'the Bondi' the official state dance? Yes, *that* Bondi." Mrs. Gray nodded.

"Hmm. Yes. I never did learn 'the Bondi,'" Principal Fleming said, shaking his head. Then he smiled and shrugged. "Well, you can't say they're not thinking outside the box. And, if I recall correctly, he did score well in the last round of state testing. . . ."

Mrs. Gray raised her eyebrows. "So Mr. Personality has a brain. Still, why couldn't they have picked a more serious student?"

"Whatever their rationale, this seems quite clear. There is to be one scholarship contestant per school. And ours"—Principal Fleming sighed, dropping the letter onto his desk—"is Bondi."

He chuckled. "God help them."

• •

Dear Scholarship Candidate:

Remember, your appointment is at 10:00 A.M. this Sunday. Doors will close at 10:01 sharp. No latecomers will be admitted. No exceptions will be made, for any reason. Any candidates not inside the room at 10:00 A.M. will be immediately disqualified.

Sunday

POST-IT Note on Melissa Burris's clock radio:

Remember—
scholarship thing
today, 10:00 A.M.
Check bus routes
first thing.
DON'T FORGET.

Three minutes to ten. Melissa stared at the ticking clock above the desk in the scholarship office downtown and tried to look like someone more together than Melissa Burris. She didn't even know why she was there. It wasn't like she was going to win the scholarship—Mrs. Orlin had told her that flat out after she'd called her up to the office a couple of days ago.

When she'd heard her name over the intercom, Melissa

had known without a doubt what it was about. She'd been dreading that moment for a long time. Someone had ratted her out for selling worksheet answers. Tommy Pittman, probably. Jerk.

She'd had her whole defense ready by the time she got to the office—it *was all a misunderstanding, it wasn't like it sounded, Tommy Pittman was a lying liar* (or, if it wasn't Tommy, then *Caitlin Jarvis was a lying liar*. Melissa was nothing if not flexible). But as it turned out, it wasn't about worksheets at all. It was actually a *good* thing for a change—she'd been picked to be in some weird scholarship competition.

Or at least it had felt like a good thing until Mrs. Orlin opened her mouth and ruined it.

"They obviously meant Melissa Burke and just got the name wrong," she'd said with a sniff, handing Melissa the letter. "Or maybe Melissa Jaffe. To be honest, *any* Melissa at Morton Middle is more qualified to represent the school than you are, Miss Burris. When I spoke with the organizers on the phone, I tried repeatedly to make them understand their error, but they refused to rectify the situation. We'll just have to make the best of it. They'll figure out their mistake soon enough. Try to look presentable, at least. And please, do your best not to embarrass the school."

Melissa cringed just remembering it. She shifted in the uncomfortable office chair in her "most presentable" outfit and tried not to fiddle with the strap of her book bag. She didn't know exactly how Mrs. Orlin thought she would embarrass the school, but fiddling with her bag probably qualified.

She just hoped no one would notice that frayed spot on the edge of her collar. She hadn't seen it until it was too late to change, but even if she had, she couldn't have done much about it. It wasn't like she was Amber Whitmore or one of those kids with a whole closet full of fancy clothes to choose from. If she was, she sure as heck wouldn't be doing worksheets for bus and lunch money.

She had to get that scholarship.

Two minutes to ten. Melissa frowned and looked around.

Aside from the tall man at the desk who was pointedly ignoring her, she was the only person in the room. And except for an abandoned messenger bag under the chair by the door, there wasn't any sign of anyone else. That was weird. Melissa was pretty sure the letter had said three competitors, but she didn't even hear anyone else in the hallway. She checked her watch. It said the same thing as the clock on the wall. One and a half minutes to ten. Melissa smiled. Maybe this was going to work out, after all.

Mothballs. That was the first thing Wilf noticed when he lurched up the final flight of stairs into the long hallway. The air had a tinge of mothball smell, with a slight whiff of peppermint. Wilf paused for a second to catch his breath, trying not to let the odors bother him. Then he launched himself down the hall toward the open door.

He thought he'd timed everything just right to get to the office by ten, but how was he supposed to know his alarm wouldn't be loud enough to wake him up? And it wasn't his fault that he didn't have any clean underwear. Well, maybe it was *kind* of his fault, since he was supposed to have put his clothes in the laundry hamper, but shouldn't his mom have noticed there was no underwear?

He hadn't been able to find his watch before he left, so he wasn't sure of the exact time, but the door being open was a good sign, right? If it was the right room. Wilf wasn't even 100 percent sure he was on the right floor.

He shouldn't have stopped for breakfast. That had been a mistake in retrospect. And he should've known the elevator would never show up. He'd thought taking the stairs would save time, but he should've remembered that liking sports didn't mean he was the athletic type who could do stairs three at a time. If he'd had to go up even one more flight, Wilf figured he probably would've just collapsed on the stairs and died.

Wilf staggered up to the doorway. "Am I too late? I'm too late, right? Is it ten yet?" His mom would kill him if he'd missed this. He never should've even told her about it, but once she'd read the fancy scholarship letter, there was no way he could skip out on the meeting. He hadn't seen her that excited about any of his school stuff in a long time. He was just glad that she didn't really expect him to win.

The mothball smell was stronger in the room—probably coming from the tall man at the desk, who was acting like he hadn't even noticed the crazy kid slam into the doorframe. One thing Wilf was sure of—the smell wasn't coming from that angry-looking red-haired girl sitting two chairs down. She was apple shampoo all the way. She glared at her watch and then back at him again.

"Five seconds to spare," the tall man at the desk said. "Quite admirable. Now, if you wouldn't mind, the door? It is ten o'clock. Time to get started."

Wilf nodded and pushed himself into a standing position. He hadn't blown it. Not yet, anyway. Five seconds was plenty of time. He still had a chance at this.

Wilf turned to close the door, only to find the doorway now occupied by a wiry black kid holding a cup of hot chocolate.

"Don't mind me," the kid said. He stepped in behind Wilf and closed the door with his foot. Then he stuck out his free hand. "So, scholarship meeting, am I right? Bondi Johnson, pleased to know you."

Wilf stared at the kid for a second, then gave his hand a loose shake. Bondi nodded at Miss Apple Shampoo and settled into the chair that had the messenger bag underneath. She didn't nod back. She just glared at the clock as though it had personally let her down.

Bondi held up his hot chocolate cup as if toasting the tall man. "Found the vending machine, just where you said it was," Bondi said, turning to nudge Wilf in the side. "I've been here awhile."

Wilf thought Miss Apple Shampoo's head was about to explode, she turned so red.

The tall man smiled anemically and got up from behind the desk. "Wonderful. Bondi Johnson, now that you've introduced yourself, may I introduce your competitors, Master Wilfred Samson and Miss Melissa Burris?"

The wiry kid, aka Bondi, nodded at Wilf and winked at Miss Apple Shampoo, aka Melissa.

"If you would be so kind, Master Samson?" The tall man gestured toward the chair next to Melissa Apple Shampoo. Wilf nodded and collapsed into it, stretching his legs far out into the room.

Wilf frowned. Maybe the mothball smell wasn't coming from the man at all—maybe it was the chair upholstery, or the cabinet next to him. But that didn't explain the peppermint. And the office didn't look like a mothball type of place—it was just your generic corporate office. But it wasn't like Wilf could do any investigating without being obvious about it. Once the meeting was over, though, he was out of there. Mothballs always did a number on him.

"Now, so we aren't disturbed . . ." The tall man glided

to the door and threw the dead bolt, locking them in. "This room is now officially sealed."

Wilf glanced at the other two kids. Miss Apple Shampoo was frowning. Even the wiry kid seemed thrown.

The tall man clapped his hands and then held them together. "I'll inform Mr. Smith that we're ready. Let the games begin."

RULES:

1. There will be no sharing of clues.
2. There will be no discussion of clues with other competitors.
3. There will be no discussion of clues with outside elements.
4. Each solution will be accompanied by photographic proof, to be provided at the time of presentation.
5. The student who provides the correct solutions first and is declared the winner shall be given a $10,000 scholarship, no more, no less.
6. These terms are confidential and shall not be disclosed to anyone for any reason, in perpetuity.
7. The Organizers reserve the right to alter or amend these instructions and/or rules at any time, without prior notice.
8. The Organizers reserve the right to issue no scholarship if they feel that these terms, or the spirit thereof, have not been met or have been violated in any way.
9. Remember, this is not a game.

The Undersigned acknowledge these rules and swear to abide by them, from now and in perpetuity. No exceptions. This contract is legally binding, and any violations thereof will be punished to the full extent of the law.

Melissa Burris

Bondi Johnson

Wilfred Samson

Melissa put down the pen and sat back down. The original letter hadn't said anything about contracts, but that one had seemed pretty straightforward at least. She knew Gran wouldn't be happy about it, though. If there was one thing her grandmother didn't like, it was contracts. But the man had been pretty clear—no signature, no scholarship. And she was going to get that scholarship. Gran wouldn't care about any stupid contract when Melissa walked in with ten thousand dollars.

Bondi signed his name with a flourish and took the papers from the tall man at the desk, flipping through them as he sat back down.

There were a bunch more rules, it looked like, and the paper was all wrong—it felt damp, it smelled funny, and the ink was this weird purple color. All except the last page, which was written out by hand and just said one thing:

Always remember:
One points you forward.
One takes you back.
One is a trick.

Bondi frowned and raised his hand. "One is a trick? What does that mean?" He didn't wait to be called on. It wasn't like they were in school—he probably hadn't even needed to raise his hand, but the tall man looked like the type who would appreciate it.

"Please do not read ahead, Master Johnson. Mr. Smith will answer your questions presently," the tall man said solemnly. "Now that we've all agreed to the terms, allow me to present him to you."

The tall man smiled at them, crossed to the inner office door, and then threw it open in a dramatic display, revealing a sour-looking, stocky man waiting in the doorway. It would've been very dramatic and creepy if the door hadn't bounced off of the wall and almost walloped Mr. Smith in the stomach.

"Thank you, Mr. . . . erm . . . Butler," Mr. Smith said, his beady eyes darting nervously as he examined the children. "As you know, you three have been invited here to compete for a very unusual scholarship, and you all have signed a legally binding agreement."

Butler coughed discreetly into his fist.

"A binding agreement," Smith said, shooting a glare at Butler. "One that will be strictly enforced, make no mistake. Let me say, first and foremost, that you were all chosen specifically for your particular, erm, *talents*."

Melissa squirmed in her seat. She wondered if she should say something about how she wasn't Melissa Burke or Melissa Jaffe. It was going to be pretty embarrassing when they realized they had the wrong Melissa.

Mr. Smith turned to stare at her, as though he'd heard her thoughts. "And those talents were not academic in nature, Miss Burris, Master Samson, and Master Johnson. Rest assured. I know what you are. You are not here by mistake."

Melissa tried to force herself to smile, but somehow hearing *I know what you are* didn't fill her with warm and fuzzy feelings. She managed to look enthusiastic until Mr. Smith turned his focus to Bondi.

"You will each be given three clues. You will keep those clues confidential, and you will provide the solutions *to me*, together with evidence that your solution is correct. Your clues are unique, so there is no possibility of cheating off of one another."

"Yep, all that was covered in that thing we signed," Bondi agreed. He wasn't buying the Smith guy's whole tough act. It was going to take a lot more than some old guy giving him the hairy eyeball to throw him off his game.

Mr. Smith continued on as though Bondi hadn't even spoken. "And let me make that point crystal clear. You will provide these solutions only to me."

Butler cleared his throat and folded his arms.

"To me, or to Mr. Butler here. The child with the correct solutions will be given a ten-thousand-dollar scholarship, assuming, of course, that all terms of the competition have been met to my satisfaction. Once the scholarship is awarded, our tenuous connections will be severed, and there will be no further contact or communication. Now, is everything understood?"

"No further contact or communication?" Melissa couldn't help herself. That just sounded weird.

"I presume you'd hoped to become pen pals, Miss Burris?" Mr. Smith said coldly.

Melissa's face turned bright red. "Well, no, but—"

"Where are the clues?" Wilf interrupted, his voice sounding rusty, like he didn't use it much. "Do you give them to us? And what kind of solutions are you talking about here? Is there going to be math, or what?"

Mr. Smith eyed him carefully, like he was a lizard trying to estimate the exact distance to a fly. "That will become apparent momentarily."

"So is it just research stuff? Or word problems, or a scavenger hunt, or something?" Wilf didn't really get what they were supposed to do. And if he had to stay there much longer, he was going to need a Kleenex.

Mr. Butler coughed into his fist again and raised an eyebrow at Mr. Smith.

Smith sighed and rolled his eyes. "Yes, of course. Allow me to elaborate, Master Samson. No, it is not math. But you *will* need to use your brain and other skills to discern the answers. To be honest, I now think it may be beyond your personal capabilities. But, as Mr. Butler reminds me, I must tell you that your needs have been accounted for. You will each have access to a nonsmoking, licensed driver who will take you to any location necessary to find the answers to your clues. Mr. Butler feels, and I must agree, that it would be unwise for you to venture out into the city entirely alone. I have provided, at great personal expense, a cell phone for each of you to use for the duration of the competition so you can summon your driver, should you need assistance. Your safety is paramount. Understood?"

"Sure, okay," Wilf said. Not really, but whatever—he was getting a phone and a driver. How awesome was that?

"Good. Butler?" Mr. Smith nodded at the tall man, who opened a desk drawer and took out three manila envelopes.

Mr. Butler handed one each to Wilf, Bondi, and Melissa.

"Now remember," Mr. Smith continued, "your clues are one of a kind. If you lose anything in that packet—your phone, your clues, anything—it cannot and will not be replaced. Any questions?"

Wilf still had a ton of questions, but he could tell the right answer was no. So he bit his tongue and kept his trap shut.

"Good." Mr. Smith's eyes gleamed. "You are dismissed. I do not expect to see you again without solutions and evidence in hand."

He turned and, without a word, marched into the inner

office, slamming the door behind him.

Mr. Butler unbolted the outer door and held it open for the kids to exit. "Best of luck to you all," he said with a cheerless grin, adding under his breath, "God knows you'll need it."

• •

REPORT

To: Mr. Smith
From: Mr. Butler

Upon receiving their clues, the three subjects exited the building without speaking to one another.

Miss Burris traveled on foot in a northerly direction, finally stopping in Daley Plaza.

Master Johnson entered a dining establishment a block from the office.

Master Samson immediately summoned Mr. Frank Jennings, driver.

All as expected.

Melissa

M elissa found an empty bench and carefully surveyed the plaza before unzipping her jacket and taking out the manila envelope. There were a ton of people around, but nobody seemed to be paying attention to her. Not the clusters of touristy people staring up at the big Picasso statue, not the guy standing next to a black car across the street, and not the group of girls scream-laughing over something on one of their phone screens.

Melissa clutched the envelope tightly and looked around one last time. Because even though nobody was paying attention to her, she had a prickly feeling on the back of her neck. A feeling like she was being watched.

A pigeon landed next to an abandoned french fry container, making her jump. Melissa laughed to herself. She was being silly. It was just a scholarship thing. It wasn't like anyone was going to be spying on her. Besides, she only had a few hours. She had to be back at three to relieve her grandmother, so she needed to use every minute to figure out her clues so she could win the money.

She opened the envelope and pulled out a thick packet of paper and a ziplock bag. She sucked in her breath. The ziplock bag had a real cell phone inside—one of the old-fashioned ones that flipped open, but still, it was a phone of her very own. The bag also held a disposable camera and what looked like a real debit card. Melissa frowned at the card. She'd heard about people getting sucked in with cards like that, buying things they couldn't afford. She didn't want to get caught in a trap.

Melissa quickly stuffed the ziplock into her pocket and scanned her surroundings again. The girls had moved on and been replaced by two businessmen, but the man across the street was still standing by the car. Melissa stared at him for a long second, but he didn't seem to be looking at her. He probably hadn't even noticed her sitting there.

Melissa zipped the pocket of her windbreaker shut and then picked up the thin letter-sized envelope that was on top of the papers. Handwritten on the front was one word: *Clues*.

Melissa eased the envelope open, and took out the three slips of paper that were inside. She read the first one.

Go to the site of Lorado Taft's Death in 1909.

Melissa examined the piece of paper for any other message, but that was it. Lorado Taft's Death. 1909. Got it. Melissa breathed a little easier. If all the clues were as straightforward as that one, she'd have this thing solved in no time. Heck, if she was lucky, she might even be done by three o'clock. Sure, she didn't know who Lorado Taft was or where he'd died, but how hard could it be to find out, right?

Melissa put that clue back into the envelope and read the next one.

Freeze! Look to the building
where Tarzan swam to find your
"Contribution."

Okay, maybe three o'clock was a little ambitious. It's not like those old guys were going to make it *too* easy. It was a scholarship prize, after all—the contest had to be a little hard. She wasn't worried, though. Tarzan was pretty noticeable, so it probably wouldn't be hard to figure out where he hung out. Melissa tucked her hair behind her ear and read the last clue.

Go to 1910 for ice cream, then
stick around to watch the newborns.

Melissa's eyes narrowed as she stared at the clue for a

long minute. Frowning, she flipped the paper over, examined it, and read it again. Finally, she tucked it back into the small envelope and stared at the pigeon, who was having some major issues with the discarded french fry container. Melissa flipped through the packet of papers, scanning the pages quickly. There had to be something that she was missing. But no, just more boring rules and lists and blah, blah, blah. She pulled the clues out of the envelope again and held the third one up to the light, but there weren't any secret messages, no hidden words that she could see. Just a regular piece of paper, with that dumb message.

Go to 1910 for ice cream, then stick around to watch the newborns.

Melissa shoved the clue back into its envelope and then stuffed everything into the packet again.

They must think she was a real idiot, an easy mark. They must think she was such a sucker. She couldn't believe she'd actually fallen for their scam.

She got up abruptly, startling the pigeon so badly that he decided to give up french fries entirely.

Stupid scholarship. The whole thing was nothing but a joke. Just a bunch of pathetic old men getting their kicks by making kids look dumb. What a bunch of losers. *Go to 1910.* What a crock.

Melissa's face burned. She was such an idiot, thinking she'd been picked for a special thing. As if someone would just give her a brand-new phone of her very own and tell her she had a shot at big money. Right. She should've known better. Things like that didn't happen in real life, especially in Melissa's life. One official-looking letter on fancy stationery was all it had taken for her to forget that.

Mrs. Orlin was going to have a great time yukking it up when she heard about this. Melissa stomped down to the bus shelter and waited, her stomach twisting into knots as she thought about school on Monday.

Wilf

Wilf gave his new phone a few test flips while he waited for his driver. It was pretty ancient looking, but it had a cool retro vibe that was kind of awesome. Wilf slid it into his jacket pocket as the sleek black car slid up to the curb. The driver, a red-faced man with a mustache and gray hair, hopped out and grinned at Wilf, hurrying around the car with his meaty hand outstretched.

"Mr. Samson, good to be working with you. My name is Frank Jennings. You can call me Frank. Or Mr. Jennings. Whichever you want. Just don't call me Francis—I hate that." The man grabbed Wilf's hand and shook it vigorously. "This is an exciting day for both of us, right, sport?" Frank winked and opened the car door for Wilf.

"Sure." Wilf shrugged as he climbed into the backseat. The upholstery was smooth leather, and there was a fresh clean smell inside the car, like oranges or fancy soap. There were even little bottles of water in the cup holders. Wilf leaned back. He could get used to this.

"So what did they tell you about this job, exactly?" Wilf asked as Frank got behind the wheel again. He wasn't sure if Frank counted as an "outside element" or not. He figured he probably didn't, but if Frank didn't know what was going on, Wilf wasn't going to be the one to tell him.

"Probably just what they told you. You've got some clues, and my job is to take you wherever you need to go to solve them. Whatever you need, just ask. Pretty sweet setup you've got here, huh, kid?" Frank smiled at Wilf in the rearview mirror. "Not like any other assignment I've had, I'll tell you that."

Wilf nodded, relieved that he wouldn't have to keep anything from Frank. He wasn't what you'd call the world's best secret-keeper; it would be just like him to accidentally spill his guts and get the boot on day one.

"Okay, now, where to? You're the boss now," Frank said, buckling his seat belt.

"Right. I'm the boss." Wilf hesitated. If there was one thing Wilf was not used to being, it was the boss. He'd never even been chosen as a team captain in gym, and that was as low stakes as you could get. He was never first choice for anything, and to be honest, he wasn't sure how he'd ended up in a competition like this one. He'd tried to figure it out, but in the end, he decided they must've picked names out of a hat or something.

Wilf chewed on his lip. "So I can tell you anywhere?"

Frank grinned. "Sure. Well, within city limits. They said nothing outside city limits. But don't you need to check that envelope first?"

Wilf felt himself turning red. He didn't figure there was any way he was going to be able to solve any of those clues, but he had to at least pretend to try if he wanted to stay in the contest. And who wouldn't want to stay in the game when it came with so many perks? "Right, so, um, maybe just drive around while I figure it out."

"You got it, boss," Frank said, pulling out into traffic.

"Boss," Wilf repeated under his breath. He dumped the

contents of the envelope onto his lap again. Once he'd gotten the packet, he'd immediately pulled out the cell phone and Frank's number, but he hadn't taken the time to look at anything else. Wilf ignored the papers—he could deal with the reading stuff later, if ever. Instead he picked up the envelope marked *Clues* and opened it, pulling out the slips inside. He examined the first one.

Jeremiah 6:23 plus Psalm 46:9

"Huh," Wilf said, shuffling that clue behind the others. Some Bible thing, it looked like. He'd figure it out later. He read the next clue.

Madame Tussaud and Mrs. O'Leary
would be proud of their little blue
friend.

"Huh," Wilf said again. That made even less sense than the first one, and it was in English and everything, not in Bible code.

"You say something?" Frank said from the front seat. "Got a destination for me?"

Wilf put the second clue back in the envelope and gave a small gasp. He really should've taken more time checking out the packet before he had called Frank. Because, in his hurry, he'd overlooked the most important thing. There was a debit card.

Oh yeah, he definitely wanted to stay in the contest.

Wilf stuffed the last clue back into the envelope without looking at it and chucked the packet onto the seat next to him. "This debit card, you know anything about that?"

"What do you mean?" Frank frowned at him. Wilf wasn't even sure Frank was the one to ask about this stuff, but he was the only one there.

"Can I use it? They won't mind, right?"

Frank gave him a funny look. "Well, yeah. It's for expenses. You know, a per diem type thing. They want a level playing field, right? So if you need money, use that," Frank said, looking at him in the rearview mirror.

"*Any* expenses?" Wilf held his breath.

"Well, don't go crazy on me. But whatever you need to do what you're doing, I guess."

Wilf's eyes gleamed. "Great." He cleared his throat. "So. How do you feel about baseball, Frank?"

Frank grinned at him and hit the gas.

Bondi

B ondi waited until the waitress brought his Coke and ice cream sundae before he ripped open his manila envelope and poured the contents out onto the table. As he expected, the cover sheet of the packet of papers was a list of the items in the envelope. He went through everything carefully, reading the guidelines and checking to make sure everything was there. Phone, check. Driver info, check. Debit card, check. Clues, check. Instructions, check.

Satisfied that he wasn't missing anything, Bondi cracked his neck (to the left, and the right), and carefully lay the small *Clues* envelope down in front of him. Then he put the papers and camera back into the manila envelope. He slipped the debit card and driver info into his pocket and picked up the phone.

"Great personal expense," Bondi scoffed. "Right." The phone looked like it might've been considered high-tech

ten years ago, but it was pretty far from up-to-date. Bondi wasn't even sure it could text. But first things first.

Bondi cracked his knuckles and opened the small envelope. He closed his eyes, pulled out the first clue, and, after taking a deep breath, read it.

Eli should've called this bubbler "Spitty Geese with Fish Huggers."

Bondi frowned as he reread the clue. *Bubbler.* That word had to be the key, he could tell. And it seemed really familiar to him.

Bondi stifled a laugh as he slapped the clue down on the table. This was going to be too easy. *Bubbler* was the key, all right. Anyone who'd had Mr. Reynolds in fourth grade had to know that a *bubbler* was another word for a *fountain.* (Other interesting Mr. Reynolds trivia: he said *jimmies* instead of *sprinkles* and *pop* instead of *soda,* and called all the guys in the class *boyo.* He also would've been an astronaut instead of a teacher if it hadn't been for his lousy 20/30 vision. Not that Bondi thought any of that would come up in this contest, but it never hurt to remember stuff.)

But if the clue was about a fountain, there was only one "bubbler" in Chicago that mattered: Buckingham Fountain in Grant Park. Bondi helped himself to a bite of sundae and grinned an ice-creamy grin. All he had to do was take a photo, and he was a third of the way to victory. Bondi put down his spoon and pulled out the second clue.

Help your bird friends get Wright to the Root of the matter as you spiral down from 12 to 2.

Bondi shrugged. Tougher, but how hard could it be? He knew lots of places that had birds. It was probably the Arboretum or something. Worst case scenario, he'd Google *birds in Chicago.* No biggie. He'd get it done.

He wiped his mouth with his napkin and took out clue number three.

Surrounded by glass, you'll find the world at your feet.

Bondi put the clue back into the envelope. He had some pretty good ideas about that already. How many places could there be in Chicago where you're surrounded by glass? Not many, probably. And according to page three of that information packet, the solutions to the clues were all inside the city limits. Piece of cake.

Bondi had always tried to keep his academic life low profile. Sure, he did well enough to keep his parents happy, but when he was at school, he wanted to be the kid other kids wanted to be, not just a brain. It might be high time to change that image a little, though. Winning this scholarship would be a pretty awesome feather in his cap. Another bright light on the Bondi marquee.

Bondi took another big spoonful of his sundae to celebrate. It wasn't often that he got ice cream, not since his mom had gotten on that weird health kick and put them all on that new Paleo diet. Heck, he might even have another sundae before he left, just as a pat on the back.

Bondi almost felt sorry for those two other kids. They wouldn't know what hit them.

SOLUTIONS TO CLUES

By: _Bondi Johnson_

1. Eli should've called this bubbler "Spitty Geese with Fish Huggers."

SOLUTION: _Buckingham Fountain, Grant Park, Chicago, IL_

2.

3.

Melissa

Melissa finished the last problem on Damon Anderson's math worksheet and tucked it into her notebook to deliver on Monday. That was good for another five bucks. It wasn't a ten-thousand-dollar scholarship, but at least it was something. It wasn't like she had a lot of options. Her bus ticket wasn't going to pay for itself.

"*Melissa!* Check it out! Right in the crotch."

Melissa rolled her eyes. Her brother, Liam, was watching some blooper show on TV, and the last video had him laughing so hard that he slid off the couch.

"Let me guess: a baseball?" It was usually a baseball on those shows.

Liam giggled and crawled back onto the couch. "Better! German shepherd. Nailed him right where it counts."

Melissa plunked down next to him. A cereal commercial was on. "Sorry I missed it."

Liam wiped his eyes and giggled one last time. "It's okay. I bet they'll show it again after the commercial. It was too awesome to show just once."

"You kids aren't watching that bloopie show again, are you?" Melissa's grandmother hurried in from the kitchen, clipping her earrings on as she walked.

"*Blooper,*" Melissa corrected her.

"That's what I said. Bloopie." She tugged on her right earring to make sure it was secure and started on the left one. "Is that what's on?"

"Yes, Gran," Liam said.

Melissa's grandmother finished with her left earring and sighed. "Well, okay, but don't watch it all day. Put something else on for a while. Try that Learning Channel for a change. TLC—that's supposed to be educational."

"Um. Okay," Liam said, giving Melissa a worried look. Their grandmother obviously wasn't a frequent viewer of The Learning Channel. Shows about extreme hoarding and weird addictions probably would be educational, but most likely not in the way her grandmother had in mind.

"I'm running late for my coffee, but I'll be back by dinner, so be good, and don't make a mess." Melissa's grandmother was on a limited income, but she had budgeted their expenses so that she and her friend Margie could splurge on a cup of coffee at the nearby McDonald's once a week. She wasn't about to miss it. "Now, don't forget— Ooh! Turn it up!"

Gran snatched the remote out of Liam's hand and cranked up the volume of the TV. An ancient-looking man in a suit was glaring at the camera.

"Enoch Ambrose," Gran breathed.

"Here we go," Liam said under his breath.

"Have some respect," Gran said, sitting down next to Melissa. "Now shush."

"Tonight at ten, Chicago Action News has the latest on the death of Enoch Ambrose, multimillionaire and founder of Ambrose Industries. He died earlier this month, leaving a will that some have described as unusual, but others say just reflects the eccentricities of its author. Initial expectations were that he would leave his vast estate to his two children, but as inside sources tell us, it may not be that simple. We'll give you an update on the execution of that will, and what might be causing the delays. Also, is your toaster oven waiting to kill you? Our I-Team Investigation says yes. Details at ten."

Gran stood up. "Why are the good ones always dead?" she said, handing the remote back to Liam. "Ah well, Margie's waiting. Watch your brother, Melissa. And don't forget—I told Mrs. Lewis you'd print out her e-mails this afternoon."

"Sure, no problem," Melissa said.

Mrs. Lewis across the hall could barely work her computer, so twice a week Melissa went over to print out any messages sent to the Lewis account. Mrs. Lewis spent the days in between perusing exciting offers from sketchy pharmaceutical companies and pen-pal invitations from Russian women who were under the misapprehension that she was a man. Melissa didn't mind doing it, though. Gran's ancient desktop had died last year, and she hadn't saved up enough to buy a new one yet. It was nice for Melissa to be able to use a computer every once in a while without having to truck all the way down to the library.

Maybe when she won the contest, she'd be able to get a computer of her own. Sure, the money was for school stuff, but maybe they'd let her use a little bit now, if she asked really nicely. Then maybe Gran could go to McDonald's with Margie whenever she wanted. And maybe Melissa wouldn't have to watch Liam all the time.

Melissa gave a short laugh. Maybe pigs would fly, too. She didn't think that Smith guy would do anything for her, no matter how nicely she asked.

"Good to see you smiling," Gran said, patting Melissa on the shoulder. She kissed Liam and Melissa, leaving red smudges on their cheeks, and picked up her purse from the table by the door.

"What's this?" she said, holding Melissa's manila envelope up in the air. "Something exciting?"

"Just for school. You know," Melissa said, trying to sound casual as she lunged for the envelope and snatched it out of her grandmother's hands. "Nothing important."

Gran cocked her head at Melissa but just nodded. "Well, take care of that 'nothing important.' And remember: Mrs. Lewis."

She smoothed Melissa's hair and then bustled out. Melissa locked the dead bolt behind her, and then stood, staring down at the envelope.

"Oh man, you missed it again!" Liam called from the living room. "Right in the crotch!"

Melissa sighed. "Hey, Liam, can you hang out for five minutes while I go print that stuff?"

"Sure." Liam peered at her from over the back of the couch. "Dead-bolt the door, and only answer the secret knock?"

"Right." Melissa clutched the manila envelope tightly. "Be back in a sec."

Melissa grabbed her keys and stepped into the hallway, waiting until she heard Liam throw the dead bolt before hurrying over to Mrs. Lewis's apartment.

The scholarship contest might be a big scam, but there was at least one more thing she could check before she gave up forever. It was worth a try, anyway.

Mrs. Lewis had her computer set up right next to the entry door, the theory being that if anyone broke in, they could just take it quickly and leave the rest of the apartment alone. Melissa waited as Mrs. Lewis's computer hummed to life, and then she logged on and printed out Mrs. Lewis's e-mails—ten spam messages, one reminder to update her virus protection, a notice about a supermarket sale, and a new pen-pal invitation, this one from a woman named Olga. While the printer was working, Melissa opened another browser window. She hesitated for a moment and, taking one last look at the clue, she typed in two words: *Lorado Taft*.

The clue had said go to where he had died in 1909. One quick Internet search should tell her where in Chicago that was. She could at least check out the place, maybe take a picture for those old losers.

Melissa scanned the results and clicked on the first one.

Lorado Taft. Born, Elmwood, Illinois, 1860;
died, Chicago, Illinois, 1936. Taft was an American
sculptor, writer, and editor, who

Melissa's jaw clenched involuntarily, and she could feel the blood rushing to her face. She read the opening lines again.

died, Chicago, Illinois, 1936.

She clicked back to the search results and read another bio. The facts were the same.

Melissa squeezed her eyes shut. Well, that cinched it. If

45

she'd ever needed proof that the scholarship was a big joke, there it was, plain as day.

The clues were impossible. She couldn't go to the site of Lorado Taft's death in 1909. Because he didn't die until 1936.

SOLUTIONS TO CLUES

By: _Melissa Burris_

1. Go to the site of Lorado Taft's Death in 1909.

SOLUTION: _Up yours._

2.

3.

Wilf

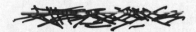

W ilf took the stairs three at a time as Frank drove away. He couldn't think of any way the day could've been more awesome, unless he'd caught that fly ball in the sixth inning. Which, technically, should've been his, since it landed right in front of him. But that little kid probably deserved to have it. And besides, as Frank had pointed out, fighting a six-year-old would've made him look pretty bad. Even if that six-year-old was a dirty thief.

Wilf stopped at his front door and made sure he'd gotten rid of the evidence—no peanut shells sticking to his cuffs or mustard on his shirt or anything. Then he headed in and dumped his backpack on the floor.

"Have a good meeting, hon?" his mom called from the kitchen. "Did you find out anything about the scholarship? I'm so proud of you."

Wilf leaned against the arched doorway to the kitchen.

His mom had everything pulled out of the refrigerator and was smelling something in a Tupperware container.

"It was fine. No big deal. They'll let us know later. I had, um, study group after."

"Oh?" Wilf's mom looked up. "Well, that's great. I'm glad you're taking your work more seriously." She sniffed the Tupperware again, and then stuck it under Wilf's nose. "What do you think? Bad?"

Wilf jerked his head back, his eyes watering. "Jeez, you have to ask? That's rank."

His mom frowned. "That's what I was afraid of. Out it goes!" She slopped the contents into the trash can and rinsed the Tupperware out in the sink.

"Yeah, so . . . study group. It was great," Wilf said, rubbing his nose to erase the stench. "We'll probably be meeting a lot, too. Every day, 'cause we've got lots of important tests and papers coming up. And, um, reports and stuff. Spreadsheets."

Wilf's mom nodded absently as she opened another container. "That's fine, hon. Oh, and you can tell your dad, too. He's supposed to call Tuesday."

"Yeah, great," Wilf said, heading off down the hallway. He closed the door behind him and immediately turned on the old laptop his dad had given him when he came through town the last time.

Wilf's dad had always traveled for his job, so he'd never

been around that much even when he was living with them. It wasn't all that different now that he and Wilf's mom had split up. Still, it would've been nice to hang out with him sometimes instead of just talking on the phone every other week. Wilf smiled to himself. His dad would've gotten a kick out of that fancy car, Wilf just wished he didn't have to wait until Tuesday to tell him about it.

Wilf flipped his new debit card in the air while he waited for the laptop to boot up. There was a whole city out there, just waiting for him. He didn't know how long this gig would last, since there was pretty much a 100 percent chance he was going to mess it all up, but until he did, one thing was certain: he was going to have a terrific time.

TENTATIVE SCHEDULE, WILF SAMSON:
1. Go to aquarium.
2. Visit Sears Tower Skydeck Ledge (Willis Tower, whatever).
3. Watch laser light show at the planetarium.
4. Go to zoo (both Lincoln Park and Brookfield, if possible).
5. Ride Ferris wheel at Navy Pier.
6. Seadog boat ride.
7. Hot Dog taste-test-a-thon—Fat Johnnie's vs. Wiener's Circle vs. Jimmy's Red Hots vs. Superdawg vs. others to be named later (until puking commences).
8. Get psychic reading.
9. Other activities yet to be determined.

SOLUTIONS TO CLUES

By: _____

1.

2.

3.

· ·

Bondi

Bondi folded his arms. "You're probably wondering why I called you here."

Inez Castillo, a little birdlike woman in glasses and a blazer, shrugged and flicked cigarette ash onto the sidewalk. "I assumed you needed a ride somewhere."

She'd pulled the black sedan up to the curb haphazardly and was leaning up against it, smoking. Bondi wasn't sure the space she was parked in was entirely legal.

Bondi nodded. "Right, I do. See, I've solved the first clue." He paused. Inez just took another drag on her cigarette. "It's a pretty big deal."

"Good for you." Inez Castillo checked her watch. "So you want to get going? I assume you've got pictures to take, or whatnot."

Bondi nodded. He thought she'd be more impressed, or at least pretend to be interested. But no reaction was fine, too. Just as long as she could get him where he needed to go, Bondi didn't care what she did.

Except for one thing.

"So . . . Ms. Castillo?" Bondi started.

"Inez is fine, kid."

"Inez. Great. The contract? It said, um, nonsmoking driver." Bondi eyed the cigarette in her hand.

Inez flicked the cigarette onto the sidewalk and crushed it with the toe of her shoe. "You see anyone smoking? No smoking here, kid," Inez said, stone-faced.

Then she cracked a smile for the first time. "So where to?"

Bondi grinned. "It's Buckingham Fountain. That's the first solution."

Inez pushed her glasses up on her nose, making her look even more like a fluffy brown bird. "Nice."

She hopped in the car and gunned the engine. "Let's win that prize."

51

Monday

Melissa's Clues:

Go to the site of Lorado Taft's Death in 1909.

Freeze! Look to the building where Tarzan swam to find your "Contribution."

Go to 1910 for ice cream, then stick around to watch the newborns.

Bondi's Clues:

Eli should've called this bubbler "Spitty Geese with Fish Huggers."

Help your bird friends get Wright to the Root of the matter as you spiral down from 12 to 2.

Surrounded by glass, you'll find the world at your feet.

Wilf's Clues:

Jeremiah 6:23 plus Psalm 46:9

Madame Tussaud and Mrs. O'Leary would be proud of their little blue friend.

???

• •

Note on Car Service Garage Chalkboard:

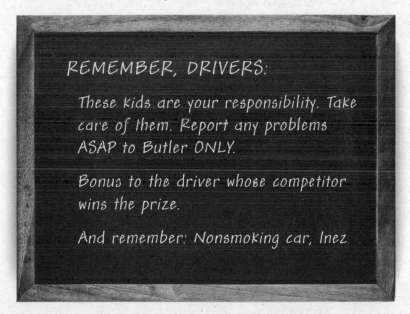

REMEMBER, DRIVERS:

These kids are your responsibility. Take care of them. Report any problems ASAP to Butler ONLY.

Bonus to the driver whose competitor wins the prize.

And remember: Nonsmoking car, Inez.

Wilf

Wilf: So what are your feelings about skipping school?

Frank: It's terrible. Leads to juvenile delinquency and the downfall of society.

Wilf: Gotcha. So I guess the aquarium's out?

Frank: I'll pick you up in 5.

Melissa

Note in Melissa Burris's Locker, Monday Morning:

Melissa,

I am *very* interested in hearing about your meeting
with the scholarship committee this past Sunday.
I will expect you in my office first thing today to
discuss any questions or requirements that you may
have had trouble understanding, and to plan your
strategy appropriately.

Your guidance counselor,

Mrs. Judy Orlin

Melissa crumpled the note in her hand as she trudged into her first-period class. She liked to think of herself as a creative person, but she couldn't come up with any excuse that would keep her out of Mrs. Orlin's office, except for oozing, festering sores, and those aren't the kind of thing you can whip up on the spur of the moment.

Melissa slid into her seat and gave a feeble wave to Tanisha Cole, who was talking a mile a minute in a monologue to Burke Cooper. "So I hardly slept at all. I mean, for *real*, I never should've started it." Tanisha paused and looked Melissa up and down. "Man, what's wrong with you? You look lousy."

Melissa didn't even know how to explain. And even if she'd wanted to, it wasn't like she could. She was pretty sure that Tanisha would qualify as an "outside element" under the contest's rule number three. "Nothing. Long story. What's up with you?"

"Oh, you have no idea. I was just telling Burke about Stephen King's *Insomnia*. It is *messed up*."

Melissa frowned. "I didn't even hear he had that. Was it on the news?"

Tanisha made a face. "Lissa, get real. It's a book? Called *Insomnia*? By Stephen King? My brother warned me not to read it, but I just had to go ahead. I don't think I slept a wink all weekend."

"Wait, what?" Melissa felt like a puzzle piece had just

fallen into place in her brain. "Holy cow."

Tanisha looked at her sideways. "Are you okay? You're acting all funny."

"No, I'm fine. Wow, that sucks. No way I'm reading that book," she said, trying to focus. Stephen King's *Insomnia*. Lorado Taft's *Death*. "Holy cow," she said again.

"You got that right. For real," Tanisha said, shaking her head. "I don't even want that book in the house with me. I had to put it out on the fire escape."

Melissa stood up abruptly. "I gotta go." She shoved her books back into her book bag and headed out, showing the crumpled note to her teacher. "Sorry, Mrs. Orlin wants to see me," she said as she hurried out the door.

Thank goodness she'd had that note. Of course, she wasn't really going to see Mrs. Orlin, but hopefully no one would figure that out.

Melissa half walked, half jogged toward the library. Students weren't supposed to just show up and use the library computers, but she didn't have much choice. No matter how much worksheet money she saved up, she wasn't getting a computer anytime soon. And Mrs. Lewis just didn't get enough e-mail to justify going across the hall again so soon. And Melissa needed to get online *now*.

"Miss Burris! Good, I was just coming to find you."

Mrs. Orlin was standing outside the office, blocking Melissa's path to the library. She had a smug smirk on her face, like she couldn't wait to find out what a disappointment Melissa was.

Melissa groaned inwardly. This was the last thing she needed. She tucked in her chin and barreled past Mrs. Orlin without saying a word.

"Miss Burris!" Mrs. Orlin barked after her.

Melissa turned and walked backwards as she talked. "Sorry, I can't discuss the scholarship with you. It's in the rules. Top secret. There was a contract and everything. I shouldn't have even told you that much. Legal stuff in perpetuity, you know." She turned back around and ducked into the library before she could see steam start coming out of Mrs. Orlin's ears.

Melissa smiled and flashed her pass to the school librarian too quickly for the librarian to see that it wasn't a library pass. She slid into a seat at one of the computer terminals as the librarian went back to her shelving. If Melissa was right, she'd been angsting for nothing. And she really hoped she was right.

Melissa opened the search engine and typed in three words: *Lorado Taft's Death*.

She smiled.

Jackpot.

ETERNAL SILENCE, Lorado Taft's Death
Eternal Silence, also known as the Statue of Death, was created by sculptor Lorado Taft in 1909 to mark

the grave of hotel executive Dexter Graves. It depicts a robed and hooded figure of Death personified, and those who dare to look into its face are said to see their own fates.

It is located in Graceland Cemetery, in Chicago.

Melissa squealed and clapped her hands together, earning her a stern shushing from a teacher browsing the stacks. She didn't care, though. It was real. It was a real thing, in a real place, which meant it was a real solution. The contest wasn't bogus, after all. She'd solved one of the clues. She was on her way.

SOLUTIONS TO CLUES

By: *Melissa Burris*

1. Go to the site of Lorado Taft's Death in 1909.

SOLUTION: *Up yours. Eternal Silence statue by Lorado Taft in Graceland Cemetery. (photo to come)*

2.

3.

. . . .

"But why, Melissa, why do we have to go to a cemetery? I don't want to. Cemeteries are gross and boring."

Melissa set her mouth in a firm line. "Because we're going, that's why. I can't leave you home alone with Gran gone, can I?"

"Sure, I wouldn't mind," Liam said hopefully.

"Wouldn't mind me getting in huge trouble, you mean," Melissa said, leaning out to see if the bus was coming. It wasn't. The wind picked her hair up and blew it sideways into her face. She pushed it away in irritation.

"Well . . . yeah." Liam snickered. "Gran would kill you."

"Thanks." Melissa rolled her eyes. She hoped the bus would get there soon. They had a solid three hours until Gran got back from her job, and if they weren't home then, Melissa would have some explaining to do.

Melissa leaned into the street again. Still no sign of the bus. She held her hair back out of her face and spat tiny bits of grit out of her mouth. The wind had picked up and it was a scoop-dirt-off-the-ground-and-throw-it-in-your-face kind of wind.

"Hey, Melissa," Liam said, tugging on her jacket. *"Melissa."*

"What?" Melissa looked down at Liam. He was staring straight ahead and talking out of the side of his mouth like he did when he was trying to be discreet.

"There's a guy, across the street. I think he's looking at us."

Melissa felt a prickle on the back of her neck. She pretended to fiddle with something in her book bag, but she peered up through her bangs to see what Liam was talking about. It didn't take her long to figure it out.

A man was standing silently next to a black car. He wasn't doing anything, just standing, and he was watching them. Melissa's eyes narrowed. She had a hunch that she'd seen this guy before. That he'd been watching her then, too. And she knew where. There was one way to find out.

"Should we run?" Liam was clutching the hem of her jacket, and Melissa didn't blame him. The guy looked like a real bullethead, a thug in a suit, and she would've been freaked out if she weren't so ticked off. Now all she had to do was make sure she was right.

Melissa shoved her tangled mess of hair out of her face and pulled the ziplock bag out of her pocket.

Liam's eyes widened. "Is that a cell phone? No way! Where'd you get *that*?"

Melissa shook her head. "It's not mine, okay? I don't even want it. Just hold on."

She dialed the phone and waited.

A phone started ringing across the street. The man next

to the car reached into his pocket, pulled out a phone, and put it to his ear.

"Melissa Burris. I was wondering when you would call." The man's voice was deeper than she'd expected, and he had an accent she couldn't identify. He stared at her from across the street without moving.

Melissa's voice sounded harsh in her ears. "Are you following us?" Which was a dumb question, because duh. But she had to ask.

"Of course. I am your driver. I go where you go."

Melissa pulled her hair into a ponytail and held it out of the wind. "I didn't call you. I don't want you here. Go away and leave us alone."

The man shook his head. "Melissa. You have a car and driver at your disposal."

Melissa tried not to look at Liam, who was staring at her with his mouth hanging open. "I don't need any favors. We're fine on the bus." Sure, the contest *seemed* to be on the level, but what if it wasn't? There was still too much that didn't make sense. A driver? A debit card? The last thing she needed was to get a huge bill when the whole competition was over.

The man sighed. "Melissa. Your competitors are using every tool they have been given. You are slowing yourself down. And my employer does not want you wandering the city alone. Your safety is of the utmost importance."

Melissa glared at Liam, then reached out and pushed his mouth closed. "We're fine. I can do this by myself."

She snapped the phone shut.

"You know that guy?" Liam said, his eyes still wide. "What's going on?"

"Never met him," Melissa said, pocketing the phone. "And I never will, if I have any say about it."

Liam crossed his arms. "Okay, give. You have to tell me. Are you a drug dealer or something?"

Now was Melissa's turn to gape. "What? Are you crazy? No!"

"Well then, what? It's not legal, whatever it is." He jerked his head at the man across the street. "You've got a cell phone and a grown-up stalker offering you rides. This is *not normal*, Melissa."

Melissa smacked him softly on the shoulder. "It's totally legal. Maybe not so normal, though." She bit her lip. "But it doesn't matter, because I can't tell you about it."

"*Melissa!* Come *on*! I tell you everything! It's not fair!"

"Seriously, I can't. It's not allowed."

Rule number three was very clear—she couldn't tell anyone, and anyone included little brothers. All it would take was one careless comment from Liam and she'd be out on her butt. She couldn't risk it.

"I would if I could, but it's a rule. I'd get in trouble if I told. BIG trouble."

Liam crossed his arms. "Melissa, seriously? *Seriously?* How many times have I kept secrets for you? You *know* you can trust me not to tell. And besides, with that guy around? I think you need some backup."

Melissa bit her lip. "You don't understand. This is big. Bigger than big. Biggest thing ever."

Liam rolled his eyes. "Bigger than your secret worksheet cheating scam? Yeah, I know where my lunch money comes from, Melissa. But have I told anyone? Nope. Have I let Gran find out how much things cost? Nope. I've kept your secret."

"What?" Melissa's eyes got wide. "How do you even know about that?"

"You're not the only one who can keep your mouth shut. I know *a lot* of secrets. What about that time you snuck Dave Madison's dog, Mr. Cupcake, into your room and babysat him for the whole weekend, even though you *know* we aren't allowed to have pets? I never said anything! Not to mention the time you forged not one but *two* permission slips for me. Thanks for that, by the way. Oh! And there was the time that you—"

"Okay, okay, I get it!" Melissa held up her hands. She didn't want to hear any more of Liam's version of *This Is Your Life*. "I'll tell you. But I'm not joking around. This is life and death. You swear not to tell, ever?"

Liam crossed his heart. "I swear."

Melissa took a deep breath. Yes, it was breaking the rules. Yes, it could get her disqualified, and if it did, she'd deserve it. But it wasn't like she'd never broken a rule before. And maybe Liam was right. Maybe she did need backup. Especially since she didn't know exactly what she was dealing with.

Melissa felt a wave of relief as the bus rolled up. She tried not to look at the man across the street as she pushed Liam toward the open bus door. "Get in. I've got a lot to tell you."

Bondi

Inez was leaning against the car when Bondi came out of the school. For all he knew, she'd been there the whole day.

"So where to, kid?" she asked, straightening up and dusting off her butt.

"Harold Washington Library," Bondi said, throwing his messenger bag into the backseat. "I need to make a list of all the bird-related sites in the city. Any ideas you have would be appreciated." He'd tried a quick Google search, but it had been amazingly unhelpful—there were way too many results, and he was pretty sure most of them didn't have anything to do with the clue, unless the clue really wanted him to buy a CD from a new folk band called Birds of Chicago.

"They've got penguins at the zoo," Inez said, getting into the driver's seat.

"Thanks. I'll put that down." Bondi didn't think there was a chance that the clue was talking about penguins in the zoo. But whatever. It was more likely than the CD idea. He'd figure it out at the library and have Inez take him to get a sundae before he headed home. She could pretend not to smoke while she waited.

Inez pulled out into traffic and drove for a few minutes before adjusting the mirror to look at Bondi. "Mind if I make a quick stop en route?"

Bondi shrugged. "It won't take long, will it?"

"Can't say. Probably won't," Inez said. Bondi didn't think she sounded very sure. He checked the clock on his phone. He didn't know how many clues those other kids had solved, but the last thing he wanted to do was waste time.

He looked up and caught Inez watching him in the

mirror. She was smirking. "Relax, kid, it'll only take a second. I need to get a parking pass from Frank."

"Okay, sure." Whoever Frank was. Bondi sat back and tried to relax while Inez navigated Lake Shore Drive and pulled into Navy Pier. "Wait, Navy Pier?" Bondi couldn't imagine why they were headed there. Navy Pier was basically an amusement park on a pier on Lake Michigan, with a Ferris wheel, rides, food stands, and lots of souvenir shops. Not the best place for research, but maybe there was a solution to a clue here or something.

"That's where Frank is. It'll only take a minute."

Inez pulled up at the pier entrance behind another black car, put her hazard lights on, and hopped out.

Bondi climbed out after her, careful to avoid the bunches of tourists wandering onto the boardwalk in their matching T-shirts.

Inez was talking to some middle-aged guy in a suit who was rummaging around in the glove compartment of his car. The tall, skinny kid from the scholarship meeting was there looking at his cell phone. When he noticed Bondi, he ambled over.

"Hey, you're Benny, right?"

"Bondi. You're Wilf?"

"Right." Wilf smiled at Bondi. "Isn't this awesome? I mean, this is just the best, right?" He was grinning so hard, it looked like his face must hurt.

Bondi nodded. "Yeah, it's great." He wished Wilf didn't look so happy. He must've solved one of the clues for sure, probably two, if he was looking that happy. Bondi felt sick. He had to get to the library.

"It's like that movie, you know? Where the kid does all the fun stuff in one day? How fun is that? We can do anything we want!"

Bondi frowned. "You mean Ferris Bueller?" He didn't see how solving the clues was anything like Ferris Bueller, but maybe he'd misunderstood.

"Right, that one." Wilf scuffed his shoe on the sidewalk. "So what have you done so far? We went to Wrigley, and the ledge at the Skydeck, and I just rode the Ferris wheel. Which was cool, sure, but not as cool as the Skydeck to be honest. Have you been there? It's awesome. Here, I took pictures." Wilf started fiddling with the phone again. "Isn't this thing cool? I can't get it to download any apps, but it has a camera at least."

"So those were for clues?" Bondi said, watching Wilf mess with the phone. The packet said that they were supposed to take pictures with the *camera*, but he wasn't sure if he should mention that to his competition. Still, he didn't want to win just because of a technicality—it wouldn't really be fair. "I think the rules said we're supposed to take the pictures with the camera, not the phone."

Wilf stared at him blankly.

"When we figure out the solutions to the clues." Bondi felt like he was speaking some strange language that Wilf didn't even know. "I think we're supposed to take the pictures with the disposable camera."

Wilf looked confused but nodded slowly. "Um, right. Clues. That's right. This isn't for the . . . I'm just . . . exploring possibilities, you know. About the clues." He held out the phone. "But see? Check it out."

Bondi squinted at the tiny phone display. "That's the Skydeck?"

Wilf nodded. "Yeah, and it's amazing. The ledge is that glass box they built on the observation deck of the Sears Tower, right? Sorry, *Willis* Tower now." He looked sheepish for a second. "But you can stand right there on a glass floor, like a hundred stories in the air. It's like there's nothing there, like you're floating or something. It's crazy!" He flipped the screen on the phone. "See, I took more. Isn't that wild?"

"Yeah, that's wild all right." Bondi felt excitement rising in his chest. "Can I see that again?" He took Wilf's phone and peered closely at the picture on the screen. Wilf really did look like he was standing on nothing, right out over the city. "It's almost like . . ." Bondi hesitated. "Like you have the world at your feet."

Wilf grinned again. "Yeah. Yeah, that's it exactly! That's a really good way to put it!"

Bondi suppressed a smile. "Yeah, I thought it might be."

"You guys ready?" Frank appeared next to Wilf and rocked back and forth on the balls of his feet.

"Sure, Frank. Good seeing you, Bondi. We've got a busy day ahead, though." Wilf smacked Bondi on the shoulder as he headed back to the car. "See you!"

Bondi smiled and waved good-bye. He couldn't stop smiling the whole way back to the car.

Inez looked at him skeptically. "Well, somebody got in a better mood. Ready for the library?"

Bondi shook his head. "Change of plans. We're going to the Skydeck. I've solved the second clue."

SOLUTIONS TO CLUES

By: Bondi Johnson

1. Eli should've called this bubbler "Spitty Geese with Fish Huggers"

SOLUTION: Buckingham Fountain, Grant Park, Chicago, IL

2. Surrounded by glass, you'll find the world at your feet.

SOLUTION: The Skydeck Ledge at the Willis Tower, formerly known as the Sears Tower, Chicago, IL

3.

Wilf

The traffic light was red, so Frank craned his head to look at Wilf sprawled on the backseat of the car.

"You sure you still want to go to the aquarium?" Frank asked.

"Well, yeah," Wilf said, surprised. Why wouldn't he want to go to the aquarium? "Don't you?"

"Yeah, I'm up for it," Frank said. "But that Bondi kid, it sounds like he's doing well at the contest. Inez said he'd already solved one of his clues."

Wilf's face clouded. "Oh man, really?" Why did that kid have to be such a brain? He'd hoped to have a couple of days more, at least.

Frank nodded. "You doing okay with yours? Your clue stuff?"

"Yeah, sure." Wilf made a face. "I'm working on it. Sort of," he added under his breath.

Frank nodded again. "Sure."

"It's harder than it looks. I'm just, you know . . . getting background information?" Wilf looked around for the manila envelope. It had slipped onto the floor and was half under the front passenger seat. He picked it up but didn't open it. "Besides, I think . . ."

Frank looked at him expectantly. A car honked at them from behind.

"Aw, shoot." Frank slammed his foot on the gas, and the car lurched forward. "So what'll it be?"

Wilf chucked the envelope onto the seat next to him. "The aquarium. I'm still working on the solutions. I'll have it figured out by tomorrow, for sure."

Frank gave him a half smile in the rearview mirror. "Whatever you say, boss."

TENTATIVE SCHEDULE, WILF SAMSON:

1. Go to aquarium.

2. Visit Sears Tower Skydeck Ledge (Willis Tower, whatever).

3. Watch laser light show at the planetarium.

4. Go to zoo (both Lincoln Park and Brookfield, if possible).

5. Ride Ferris wheel at Navy Pier.

6. Seadog boat ride.

7. Hot Dog taste-test-a-thon—Fat Johnnie's vs. Wiener's Circle vs. Jimmy's Red Hots vs. Superdawg vs. others to be named later. (until puking commences).

8. Get psychic reading.

9. Other activities yet to be determined.

ALSO: FIGURE OUT CLUES AND SOLUTIONS.

SOLUTIONS TO CLUES

By: _____

1.

2.

3.

• •

Melissa

L iam chewed on the string from his jacket hood. "Okay, so in my head, I know that we need to go into the cemetery. But my feet just don't want to do it."

They'd had the whole back of the bus to themselves,

so Melissa had spent the first half of the bus ride telling Liam about the contest, and the second half swearing him to secrecy.

He'd thought the contest sounded cool on the bus, but now that they were actually there, Liam was having a hard time getting past the whole cemetery thing.

"You know I can't leave you alone," Melissa said, grabbing his sleeve and physically dragging him through the gates. "Besides, it'll take two seconds. We'll run in, get the picture, run out."

Melissa hoped she sounded convincing. They were getting a photo of Death. It didn't sound promising no matter how you sliced it.

Liam made his feet like lead. "Melissa, no. This is a really bad . . . whoa . . ." he trailed off, but Melissa didn't complain. She had stopped, too.

She'd seen cemeteries before, sure. And to be honest, she'd never been all that impressed. Bunch of gray stones with bushes and fake flowers, pretty much, not to mention the dead people. But then, she'd never been to Graceland Cemetery.

Stretched out in front of them were rolling grassy hills covered with trees, ancient gravestones, and elaborate monuments big enough to be apartments. Wide paved paths branched out in three directions. The place went on as far as the eye could see.

Melissa's heart sank. This place was huge. How were they supposed to find one grave among so many, even if it was a special one?

Liam nudged her in the ribs. "I bet that's the office. Think they have a map or something?" He pointed to a small brick building off to the side.

Melissa sighed in relief. "Maybe give us directions, at least. Because, holy cow."

Liam nodded. "You said it. Holy cow."

Melissa took a deep breath and pressed the CALL button on the front door of the brick building, fingering the money in her jacket pocket as she waited. She had the ten dollars from the worksheets she'd done over the weekend, but that was all. If there was an admission fee, it was going to be a problem. The door buzzed, and she pushed it open for Liam, putting on her most appealing and innocent face.

The lady behind the desk didn't seem grouchy about them being there, and she didn't ask for money or anything. She was practically twitching, she was so excited to see them. Melissa had barely gotten the words *map* and *Dexter Graves* out of her mouth before the lady sprang into action.

"Dexter Graves? Oh sure, that's a good one. Now, here you go." She whipped out a small folded map and marked an X on the page. "You just take Evergreen until you hit Main Avenue—you can't miss it. Oh, and if you like Lorado Taft, you'll have to visit Victor Lawson's grave, although he's in a ways, on Main before you hit Woodlawn. But it's a knight statue—you should definitely see that! Oh, and if you like baseball, you'll have to check out William Hulbert, too. He was the founder of the National League, and his is shaped like a— Well, I'll let it surprise you, but I think you'll love it! They're all right here on the map."

Liam looked at the map in shock. "There are streets? With names?"

Melissa pocketed the map gratefully. "Thanks, that's terrific. We'll be sure to find it now."

"Just make sure you're back before we close the gates. Don't want you getting stuck in here!" the lady chirped.

"No, ma'am," Liam said, looking at her in horror.

"We'll be back," Melissa said, pushing Liam ahead of her out the door.

"It's so quiet here," Liam whispered after they'd been walking up the street marked *Evergreen* for a few minutes. "It's like we're not even in the city anymore. I think . . . I think I saw a coyote."

Melissa just nodded. She'd seen it, too. And there didn't even seem to be anyone else there. Just them. Well, them and the coyote.

When the road branched, Melissa checked the map and started up Main Avenue. But she'd only taken a few steps when Liam stopped in his tracks.

"I . . . I think that's him. Death, I mean," he said,

pointing off into the distance. Melissa looked up, catching her breath.

There was no mistaking that statue. *Eternal Silence.* Death.

The hooded figure stood alone in the grass, and time and the elements had weathered the statue until it was a deep green color. All except the face. The small area of Death's face that was shielded by the hood was still deep black.

Melissa shuddered. "You know, I read that if you look into his face you can see your fate."

"Just take the picture. I don't want to know my fate," Liam said softly.

Melissa hesitated, then snapped the photo. She didn't think she wanted to know her fate, either.

Melissa pocketed the camera and nudged Liam. "Well, that's it. See? That barely took any time at all. We can head back now."

Liam didn't answer. They both just stared at the statue. "If you want . . ." Melissa added, "we've still got some time before Gran gets home."

Liam looked at the ground. "Maybe we should see that baseball guy's grave before we go. You know, since we're already here. I mean, if you want to."

Melissa nodded. "And that knight guy. We should at least check that out."

Liam grinned. "Come on."

They consulted the map and then headed deeper into the cemetery.

Wilf

Wilf pushed the piles of accumulated junk to the side to clear a space on his mattress, and then he dumped out the contents of his packet.

His mom was out at one of her movie nights, leaving Wilf to his own devices. Again. Not that he minded—he was pretty much used to it. His mom wanted him to think she was with Linda, the lady from her pottery class, but Linda smelled like baby powder and cats, and whoever his mom had been going to movies with smelled like Old Spice. He guessed his mom would introduce them at some point. Wilf just hoped it wasn't Mr. Podrecki from fifth-period science. He smelled like Old Spice, too.

Wilf sifted through the papers and found the clue envelope. He was pretty sure there'd been an easy clue in there. All he had to do was solve one, and Frank would get off his back and go back to doing the fun stuff. At least for a little while. Heck, Frank should just be relieved that Wilf hadn't already been eliminated for something or other.

Wilf pulled out the first clue and smoothed it out. He hoped the crumpling wasn't a big deal—he hadn't put it back into the envelope as carefully as he'd thought.

Wilf peered down at the old-fashioned writing.

Jeremiah 6:23 plus Psalm 46:9

That was definitely Bible stuff, so that meant pretty much one thing. Copying onto a piece of paper. This one would be a cinch.

Wilf found the Bible his grandparents had given him buried on the bottom shelf of his bookcase, and he flipped through it until he found Jeremiah. It was kind of weird that the clue had two passages listed. But whatever, he could write down two quotes as easily as one. At least this wasn't going to take a lot of legwork.

Wilf stopped flipping. He'd finally found it. Jeremiah 6:23.

> "They are armed with bow and spear;
> they are cruel and show no mercy.
> They sound like the roaring sea
> as they ride on their horses;
> they come like men in battle formation
> to attack you, Daughter Zion."

Wilf blinked. Well, okay, sure. That made absolutely zero sense. But he carefully wrote it down in his notebook and then, after reading it again, turned to the Psalms section and zeroed in on Psalm 46:9.

He makes wars cease to the ends of the earth.
He breaks the bow and shatters the spear;
he burns the shields with fire.

Wilf stared at the passage for a long minute and then copied it carefully into his notebook, checking to make sure he'd gotten it exactly right. Wilf bit his lip. Sounded like some kind of before-and-after situation, with all that fighting and then not fighting, but that was the only thing that jumped out at him. There had to be something he was missing, right? This couldn't be all there was.

Wilf studied both parts again, and double-checked the clue. Nope, that's exactly what it said—those two quotes. So that's what he'd give them. Wilf lay the Bible on the bed and carefully took a photo of each of the passages with the disposable camera. It would've been easier to find them online and print them out, but if it was photos they wanted, it was photos they'd get.

Wilf closed his notebook with satisfaction. Done. At least he had one clue out of the way. Heck, he might even

do a little more research before he went to bed. It felt good
to be productive.

SOLUTIONS TO CLUES

By: WILF SAMSON

1. Jeremiah 6:23 plus Psalm 46:9

SOLUTION: JEREMIAH 6:23 AND PSALM
46:9. THEY'RE IN THE BIBLE. (ANY BIBLE
PROBABLY WORKS, BUT DEFINITELY IN THE NEW
INTERNATIONAL VERSION.)

2.

3.

TENTATIVE SCHEDULE, WILF SAMSON: (UPDATED)

1. Go to aquarium.

2. Visit Sears Tower Skydeck Ledge (Willis Tower, whatever).

3. Watch laser light show at the planetarium.

4. Go to zoo (both Lincoln Park and Brookfield, if possible).

5. Ride Ferris wheel at Navy Pier.

6. Seadog boat ride.

7. Hot Dog taste-test-a-thon—Fat Johnnie's vs. Wiener's
   Circle vs. Jimmy's Red Hots vs. Superdawg vs. others to
   be named later (until puking commences).

8. Get psychic reading.

ALSO: Figure out clues and solutions
9. Go skydiving.
10. Take helicopter tour.
11. Kayak on Chicago River.
12. Play bubble soccer (first, figure out what
    exactly bubble soccer is).

Notes on Car Service Garage Chalkboard:

2 clues solved! My kid is going to wipe
the floor with your kids. —Inez

My kid is a big-picture guy.
A come-from-behind kid.
You watch out. —Frank

My kid rides the bus. —Dimitri

Bondi

> **Bondi:** Hey, Mom and Dad, any ideas where I might do a little bird-watching in the city? It's that scholarship thing. Thanks!

> **Mom:** Maybe at the Arboretum? Or how about the zoo? They have penguins there. 😘

> **Dad:** I don't think they have penguins at the zoo anymore. But try the aquarium—I think there are penguins there.

> **Mom:** No penguins? And they call themselves a zoo?

> **Dad:** Hey, don't shoot the messenger. I'm pretty upset about it myself. 😠

Mom: I'm going to have to write a letter to our alderman. This no-penguins nonsense should not be allowed to stand. 🐧

Bondi: Pretty sure it's not penguins, guys.

· ·

Wilf

Wilf: 3 cheers for me, I solved my first clue! So, hot dog taste test on for tomorrow?

Frank: Congrats, kid! First dog's on me.

Bondi

Note Slipped Under Bondi's Door:

> Have to head out for an early meeting tomorrow, but I wanted to make sure you had this—looks like your dad was right. No more penguins at Lincoln Park Zoo. But they have other (lame, non-penguin) birds, and the aquarium has penguins galore. I've starred the most likely bird possibilities.
>
> Have fun with your new pelagic friends!
>
> Mom

ANIMAL HOUSES AND EXHIBITS,
LINCOLN PARK ZOO

☆ Regenstein African Journey
☆ McCormick Bird House
☆ Regenstein Birds of Prey Exhibit
Helen Brach Primate House
Kovler Lion House
Kovler Seal Pool
☆ Nature Boardwalk
☆ Pritzker Family Children's Zoo
Regenstein Small Mammal-Reptile House
☆ Hope B. McCormick Swan Pond
☆ Waterfowl Lagoon
Regenstein Center for African Apes
Antelope and Zebra Area
☆ Farm-in-the-Zoo
Regenstein Macaque Forest

Melissa

Melissa slid Mike Crosby's completed algebra homework into her book bag as her grandmother settled on the couch with a bowl of popcorn and the remote.

Melissa plopped down next to her. "What are we watching?"

Gran eyed her suspiciously. "You've finished your homework? All of it?"

Melissa nodded. *And Mike Crosby's and Tyler Blake's and Alissa Grant's, too,* but she wasn't about to say that. "All done."

Gran gave a tiny harrumph and tucked an afghan around her legs. "I'm watching a *Chicago Action News* Special Report—'Enoch Ambrose: The Early Years.' Nothing you'd be interested in, I imagine." Gran eyed her expectantly.

Melissa shrugged. "I could watch that. Beats that blooper show Liam's always watching."

Gran stifled a snorty laugh. "Well, okay, then."

The *Action News* I-Team was doing a report about how your mouthwash could kill you. "Should be on after this." Gran leaned in conspiratorially. "Have to admit, I always did have a tiny little crush on Enoch Ambrose. Such a looker. And what a card! He was a billionaire, you know, and an important man, but such a trickster! He was always doing a little something you'd hear about, pulling a prank on one of those other newspaper or manufacturing tycoons. They'd get so mad! They probably won't get to that until part two or three, though." She sighed and looked sadly at the fruit bouncing around in the commercial. "Such a shame. The good ones always die young."

Melissa watched as the fruit disappeared and was replaced by a photo of Enoch Ambrose. "How young was he?" she asked doubtfully. *Young* wasn't exactly the word she would've used to describe the man.

"Ninety-eight. Such a waste." Gran sighed again and ate a piece of popcorn.

"Wow. That young, huh?" Melissa waited, but Gran didn't bite. So she leaned back and watched Enoch Ambrose in the early days, when people apparently liked to dress their little sons in frilly white dresses and put bows in their chin-length hair. "So he wasn't born in say, 1910?"

Gran shot her a look. "Well, congratulations on your math prowess. No, he wasn't born in 1910, Melissa."

"Oh." Melissa made a face. She didn't know why she was still obsessing about that impossible 1910 clue. It was obviously a hoax and a big stinking joke, but still, a big part of her wanted to figure it out. As if it *could* be figured out . . .

Enoch Ambrose was riding a pony around a grassy field in some shaky ancient footage. At least there was some action—a blurry home movie of a pony was way better than another montage of black-and-white photographs. Melissa had a feeling she wasn't going to be tuning in for "Enoch Ambrose: The Teen Years."

Melissa waited for a commercial break and then nudged her grandmother. "So let's say you wanted to have ice cream in 1910. Where would you go?" Maybe figuring out the clue was just a matter of asking the right person. The rules didn't say you couldn't ask questions. And nobody was closer to 1910 than Gran. Well, nobody Melissa knew, anyway.

"Where would I go?" Gran looked thoughtful. "Well, 1910, I suppose."

"Right." Not an option. Melissa crammed the last of her popcorn into her mouth and chewed mournfully.

Tuesday

Melissa's Clues:

Go to the site of Lorado Taft's Death in 1909.

Freeze! Look to the building where Tarzan swam to find your "Contribution."

Go to 1910 for ice cream, then stick around to watch the newborns.

Bondi's Clues:

Eli should've called this bubbler "Spitty Geese with Fish Huggers."

Help your bird friends get Wright to the Root of the matter as you spiral down from 12 to 2.

Surrounded by glass, you'll find the world at your feet.

Wilf's Clues:

Jeremiah 6:23 plus Psalm 46:9

Madame Tussaud and Mrs. O'Leary would be proud of their little blue friend.

???

Bondi

Bondi went over his list of possible bird locations one last time. He'd compiled it the night before and cross-referenced it by likelihood, bird type, and potential proximity to clocks. It was a big list, and checking all the possibilities was going to take time. Time he didn't have. Especially since he wasn't sure what he was looking for.

He reread the clue one more time before sliding it into the inside pocket of his jacket. It wasn't like he needed to, though—he could recite it in his sleep.

Help your bird friends get Wright to the Root of the matter as you spiral down from 12 to 2.

The bird part was the biggest clue, but he was pretty sure *12 to 2* was a clock reference. It must be some kind of code. Once he found the clock with birds, it would all make sense. But so far his search for *bird clock Chicago* hadn't led him to anything but a bunch of online stores.

Inez was just unwrapping a piece of nicotine gum when Bondi came out of his building. "So what's the plan for today?" She tossed the wrapper into the nearest trash can as she talked. "Library again after school? You're a wild one, I'll give you that."

Bondi grinned. "Nah, not today. How about the Arboretum? I'm looking for birds."

Inez shook her head. "No dice. Outside of city limits. Got a second choice?"

Bondi frowned. He couldn't believe he'd forgotten about the city-limits rule. Now he'd need to rethink the whole thing. All that time, wasted.

Bondi looked at his list again, his shoulders sagging. "You don't happen to know any famous bird clocks around here, do you?" he asked finally, refolding his notes and putting them into his messenger bag.

"What, like a cuckoo clock?"

"I don't know." Bondi shrugged. "Maybe."

Inez gave a harsh barking laugh. "Not a big fan of birds or clocks, to be honest."

Bondi nodded like it wasn't important. "Okay, well, thanks. Just asking." He chucked his bag onto the backseat. He'd review his list on the way to school. Maybe he should check out the penguins, since everyone seemed so hot on them. The aquarium was within the city limits, at least.

Inez leaned against Bondi's door and tapped on the window until Bondi rolled it down.

Inez peered at him through the window. "I don't know about any birds, but that Marshall Field's clock on State Street is pretty famous. It's a clock, at least. And there's another big one on the Wrigley Building."

"Sounds good," Bondi said. Those clocks weren't even on his list.

Inez's mouth twitched into an almost-smile. "I don't know if there'll be anything to it. It's not like I know your answers, okay? But they're clocks." She checked her watch. "Want to try to make it before school?" She held up her hand expectantly.

Bondi leaned out of the window and gave her a half-hearted high five. "You bet I do."

"Great. Let's roll." Inez hopped into the front and buckled her seat belt.

Melissa

Melissa leaned out into the street to see if the bus was coming. It wasn't. Of course.

Liam had been completely wired after the trip to the cemetery, and he'd stayed up talking about it forever. Which seemed fine at the time, but now Melissa realized what a mistake it had been. They'd all overslept, even Gran, and they'd missed their bus and the backup bus. If the next bus didn't come soon, she might as well skip school, that's how late she'd be. But she couldn't, not with Mike Crosby's and Tyler Blake's and Alissa Grant's homework in her notebook. She wasn't about to give that fifteen dollars back.

"And remember that pyramid one? Wasn't that cool? When I die, I want a pyramid-shaped tomb. Or maybe one like a baseball, like that guy's." Liam picked up where he'd left off at breakfast, as though he'd never stopped talking. "Or my own little island, like that one across the bridge—wasn't that awesome, Melissa? Can I have one of those?"

"Sure," she said, chewing on the end of her ponytail. Still no bus. No bus, no sign of a bus, nothing that even looked like a bus. Well, that was it. She was super late for sure. Maybe even miss-homeroom-and-first-period late. Liam still had a chance of being on time, though.

"And that statue of the girl in the glass box . . . that was the creepiest thing ever."

"So creepy," Melissa agreed absently, watching a truck back out into the street, bringing traffic to a halt. She felt waves of panic rising in her chest. If it blocked the bus, she might just freak out. But there was no bus to block, so it didn't even matter. She didn't care whether the people in the Honda had to sit there waiting all morning.

Melissa chewed on her ponytail for a minute more before realizing that Liam had stopped talking. She dropped her ponytail and looked at him. "What?"

"Your guy is back," Liam said, jerking his head toward the other side of the street in a completely unsubtle attempt to be subtle. The man in the suit was standing beside his car, waiting.

Melissa scowled. "Forget it." She wished he would just go away. How creepy was that, following them around all the time, just because he was supposed to be driving her places. Whatever, weirdo, doing his job.

She looked at her watch. They were *so* late.

Three more not-buses zipped by. Melissa bit her lip and then shook her head again. "Forget it," she said mostly to herself.

The sound of the phone ringing made her jump. Liam looked at her pocket like it had a wolverine inside. "Is that you? Is that your *phone*?"

Melissa scowled harder and pulled the phone out. She didn't recognize the number, but it wasn't like she couldn't figure out who it was. "What?" she snapped.

"You are going to be late for school."

"So what? I don't care. Who cares?" Melissa said, deliberately turning her back on the man and his car. She hesitated. "Besides, I read the rules again. They say 'No extra passengers. No exceptions.' It was in the packet."

The man didn't respond.

Melissa took a deep breath. "Liam's an extra passenger. I'm not losing this thing because I broke one of the rules."

The phone went dead. Melissa stared at the screen for a minute and then shoved it back into her pocket. What a jerk. She'd been right not to trust that guy. She knew those sketchy scholarship people were no good. She shouldn't trust any of them. Just look at what they'd done with that stupid 1910 clue.

She was just leaning out to look for the bus again, when the black car pulled up in front of her and the driver hopped out, quickly circling around the car and opening the back door.

"Dimitri Omar, at your service," the man said, extending his hand to Liam. "I am an acquaintance of your sister's."

"Melissa?" Liam considered the man's hand and then tentatively shook it. Then he looked from the plush interior of the car to his sister. "Can we?"

"Of course not. Don't be silly."

Dimitri Omar didn't say anything. He just remained standing by the open door.

"It's breaking the rules, though, right?" Melissa asked finally. "I mean, it wasn't on that contract I signed, but it said in the packet 'no extra passengers.' I'll be disqualified or something, right?"

Dimitri Omar shook his head. "There is no extra passenger here. You two come as a set, no? If there is one thing I have learned, it is that you do not break up a set."

Melissa looked at her watch again. So, so late. "But are you sure? It didn't say anything about sets. Is this a trick? Are you tricking me?"

Dimitri Omar looked solemn. "I am your driver. You can trust me. I would not trick you to make you lose." He paused. "I want to win, too. You win; I win."

Melissa raised an eyebrow at him and looked back at her watch.

Dimitri stood by the open door.

Melissa looked back up the street for the bus that still wasn't coming. Then she looked back at the car and broke into a tentative smile. "Yeah. Yeah, okay. Hop in, Liam." She helped her brother climb into the car and then hesitated. "Hey, you don't know how to get ice cream in 1910, do you?"

Dimitri Omar gave a small shrug. "You go to ice cream shop?"

Melissa rolled her eyes and got into the backseat.

• •

Wilf

Wilf spread out in the backseat of Frank's car, resting his backpack on the high peaks of his knees. "Just thought you should know I solved a clue last night. Pretty awesome, if you ask me."

"Yeah, that's what you said. Way to go, champ!" Frank smiled as he pulled out into traffic. "What was it?"

Wilf flicked his hair back nonchalantly. "Well, it was these two Bible verses, see? So I looked them up and wrote them out. I took a picture and everything. One was in Jeremiah, and one was in Psalms."

Frank's smile flickered for just a second. "Well, like I said, that's great."

"It was a pretty easy one," Wilf said, looking out the window.

Frank drove in silence for a minute. "So what did they mean, do you think?"

Wilf frowned. "The Bible verses?"

Frank glanced at him in the rearview mirror. "Yeah. I mean, they must stand for something, right?"

Wilf slumped in the seat, making his knees poke up even higher. He'd thought he'd done it right, writing the stuff out just like they said, but maybe he was missing something? It hadn't said anything about the quotes meaning anything, but maybe he should've just known. He probably shouldn't have even bothered working on the clues. Then he wouldn't look like an idiot if he did it wrong. "I don't know. I couldn't figure it out. Why, you think that's important?"

Frank shook his head. "No, just curious, that's all." He forced a smile. "Hey, don't look so gloomy, clue-solver! So where to today? Still hot dogs?"

Wilf sat up straighter. "Oh yeah. Hot dog tour commence."

Bondi

Bondi stood underneath the clock at the old Marshall Field's building, staring up at it. He wished he were about five feet taller. Or at least as tall as that Wilf kid. That would be a huge help.

Inez dug a cigarette packet out of her shoulder bag, discovered it was empty, then crumpled it up and tossed it into the trash. "So, anything? Birds? Platypuses? Anything with a beak up there?"

Bondi shook his head. There were swirly curlicues on the metal, which had turned green over time, but nothing that looked like a bird, and the three sides of the clock were pretty plain—just Roman numerals. He could stare at it all day, but he had to face facts. "I don't think this is it." The Wrigley Building clock hadn't been very promising, either. Granted, it had been a lot higher up, but there didn't seem to be anything birdlike about it.

Bondi couldn't believe he hadn't found it yet. How hard could it be to find one bird clock? His parents would've both figured it out by now, he was sure of it. They'd won lots of scholarships and things when they were in school. He didn't know what was wrong with him. This whole contest should've been a snap.

Bondi gave the clock one last once-over and then walked back to the car.

"Tough break, kid. You'll find it, though." Inez checked her watch. "Ready for school?"

Bondi shrugged halfheartedly as he flopped down onto the seat. "I think we're going to have to go to the zoo, Inez. That must be it. First thing after school."

"Right. Gotcha," Inez said. "Or the aquarium. That's where the penguins are, you know."

Bondi groaned.

Melissa

Melissa couldn't believe how her day had turned around. Thanks to Dimitri Omar's fancy driving, they'd dropped Liam off and she'd made it to school with three minutes to spare. The ride to school was actually amazingly short when she didn't have to stop at what felt like every single bus stop in the city. And the best part was that she hadn't had to put up with some weirdo dripping on her the whole way. Melissa always seemed to end up next to someone with moisture issues. She just hoped her good luck would hold.

It wasn't until third-period history that her regular life kicked back in. Mr. Masterson kept eyeing her all through their pop quiz and silent reading, just like he had the first week of school. That time she'd gotten a lecture about speaking up in class and overcoming her "paralyzing shyness." Because calling out a student in class is the perfect way to make her feel more comfortable.

Melissa tried to ignore him and focus on her book until the bell rang. She'd almost made it out of the classroom, when Mr. Masterson called her name.

Melissa stopped in the doorway. She really didn't want to turn around, but it wasn't like she had a choice. Since he was the teacher and all.

"Yeah?" She tried not to sound surly. She had a problem with that sometimes. Just ask Mr. Masterson.

"Melissa, could I speak to you for a moment?" Mr. Masterson was still sitting at his desk, staring at her with his most serious I'm-here-to-help expression.

Melissa's good mood took a nosedive into the pit of her stomach. Well, it had been nice while it lasted.

"Sure. What is it?" Melissa drifted back in front of his desk. She hoped he wasn't going to suggest she take martial arts again. That had been his recommendation last time. He'd said it would boost her confidence. It was too bad she hadn't done it—a well-placed karate chop would be just the thing in this situation.

"Melissa . . ." Mr. Masterson looked at the blotter on his desk. "I don't quite know how to say this . . . so I'll just say it. I went over the homework while you all were doing your silent reading today. You know that, right?"

"Yeah," Melissa said. What, did he think she was an idiot? How could she *not* know that? A cold feeling started to creep over her. It wasn't her shyness this time. It was the worksheets. She knew it. He'd figured out that she'd been doing other people's homework.

She braced herself. She was going down for sure.

"Melissa . . ." Mr. Masterson hesitated again. For someone who was *just saying it*, he was having a heck of a time spitting it out.

"Melissa," he started again, "when I looked at your worksheet, I noticed certain . . . *similarities*, shall we say, with Tyler Blake's paper. They were identical, in fact."

The cold feeling had spread all over Melissa's body and rooted her to the ground. She couldn't even feel her feet.

She'd gotten sloppy. She usually tried to mix things up when she did other kids' homework, varying the words and phrases to make it seem like the worksheets had been written by different people. But she hadn't been thinking about that when she did Tyler's last night. Like an idiot, she'd been thinking about 1910.

Melissa's mouth was so dry that it was hard to force any words out. "Really?"

"Yes. And I don't think it's a coincidence. Melissa, I hate to ask you this, but did you copy from Tyler's paper? I just want you to be honest with me. Please."

Melissa's jaw dropped. "No."

Mr. Masterson shook his head. "I'm not going to be angry if you did. If you're struggling, I want to get you the help you need. But I can't help you until you admit that you copied Tyler's work."

The cold feeling was immediately replaced by a wave of heat so strong Melissa was surprised it didn't knock her forward. She clenched her hands but tried to keep her face blank. "I didn't copy from Tyler."

Mr. Masterson looked disappointed. "You're saying it's just a coincidence that you and Tyler phrased your answers exactly the same way?"

"I guess so," Melissa said. "Is that what Tyler said? Did he say I copied?"

Mr. Masterson sighed. "Melissa, I didn't want to embarrass you by mentioning this to Tyler. Right now your grades are fine, but I don't want you to drop behind. There are tutoring sessions every day after school. I can add you to the list, and you'll be back up to speed in no time."

Melissa focused on the spot in between Mr. Masterson's eyebrows. She didn't want to look him in the eye. "I watch my brother after school. Sorry."

Mr. Masterson nodded. "Well, the offer stands. And, Melissa, I don't want to have to talk to you about this again. Consider this your one and only warning." He hesitated. "Melissa, is there something you want to talk about? Should I give you a note to see Mrs. Orlin in guidance? I'm sure she'd be happy to discuss any problems you might have."

Melissa gritted her teeth and started to shake her head.

But instead, she looked Mr. Masterson straight in the eye. "There is one thing I'd like to ask you, Mr. Masterson."

He smiled at her. "I thought so. Go ahead. I'm here for my students."

"Good, because this is important." Melissa smiled. "It's about ice cream. In 1910. How can I get some?"

To: Judy Orlin
From: Kyle Masterson
Subject: Problem Student Alert

Judy,

I think you may want to talk to one of my seventh-grade history students, Melissa Burris. She seems to be breaking down emotionally. I tried to have a friendly conversation with her about some problems with her work, and she started spouting nonsense about ice cream and the early 1900s. Then she laughed like a loon. I'm very concerned.

Kyle

To: Kyle Masterson
From: Judy Orlin
Subject: RE: Problem Student Alert

Kyle,

Thank you for reaching out. Believe me, Miss Burris
is already on my radar. I'm not surprised to hear
that she's doing subpar work and acting out. She is
involved in an academic contest that's way beyond her
capabilities, and it's having a negative effect on her—
not that she was ever Miss Congeniality to begin with.
I'm doing what I can, but I'm afraid some students are
beyond help. Watching people fail is never easy, Kyle. I
wish us both luck.

Best,
Judy

Wilf

Wilf's mouth started watering as soon as Frank pulled the car up in front of Portillo's. This was going to be the best day ever. Wilf's mom never wanted to stop for hot dogs, especially at the places he wanted to go. Like the Wiener's Circle, number two on his list, where the people behind the counter berated you when you ordered. This was going to be great.

"Hope you didn't have a big breakfast," Frank said, getting out of the car.

"Are you kidding me? I have been planning this *forever*. My dad always promised to do it with me, but, you know . . ." Wilf trailed off. "Job stuff."

"Well, I am *excited*!" Frank said enthusiastically. "This is going to be a day to remember."

He looked at the list of hot dog places Wilf had given him. There were ten mentioned specifically, and Frank had strict instructions to stop at any stand they passed that wasn't on the list. "We'd better get started. You're going to be eating an awful lot of hot dogs today."

Wilf's stomach growled. "That's what I'm counting on."

• •

Bondi

POSSIBLE BIRD / CLOCK LOCATIONS
by Bondi Johnson

   1. ZOO

      Advantage: Lots of birds

      Drawback: No known clock

      Conclusion: Investigate

   2. Alexander Calder Flamingo Sculpture

      Advantage: Named after a bird and famous

      Drawback: Doesn't really look like a

bird. Also, no clock.
Conclusion: Iffy
3. Aquarium
   Advantage: Penguins
   Drawback: Penguins
   Conclusion: Need I say more?
4. Pet Stores
   Advantage: Lots of birds
   Drawback: Too many pet stores in the
   city. Also, super-lame idea.
Conclusion: Oh man, I am going to lose
lose lose.

Bondi stared into his Tupperware container and sighed. It almost didn't seem worth the effort of lifting his fork. He pushed it aside and spread his notes in front of him on the cafeteria table. He was so close—he had just one clue left, and he had to figure it out *now*. That Wilf guy didn't seem like he was going to be a problem, but Bondi didn't like the looks of that girl with the red hair. She could be serious competition.

He had his after-school strategy almost all mapped out when his friends Jamal and Andrew plopped down into the seats next to him.

Jamal bumped shoulders with Bondi. "Buddy, come on. Put the books away." He bumped Bondi again and then leaned his chair back so it was balancing on two legs.

"Seriously," Andrew said, stuffing a soggy french fry into his mouth. He flipped Bondi's notebook shut. "You've got to pace yourself. Study too much too early in the year, and your brain will explode before Christmas."

Jamal nodded in agreement, overbalancing and slamming his chair back down onto all four legs with a jolt. "It's true. I've seen it happen."

Bondi gave a half smile. "Yeah, sorry. It's this scholarship thing. I'm not even supposed to talk about it. Once I've won, I'll have loads of time. I promise."

Jamal ate a handful of Andrew's fries. "Yeah, well, you better win soon, okay?"

Andrew smacked his hand away. "Yeah, what are you waiting for? Don't want the other kids to feel bad?"

Bondi groaned. "I am *so close*. You have no idea. Just one step away."

Andrew grinned. "That's what I like to hear!" He pulled Bondi's Tupperware over and pried the lid off. "Now what have we got—?" He wrinkled his nose and looked up at Bondi. "What the heck is this?"

Bondi grabbed the container from him and put the lid back on. "Nothing. Chard. With golden raisins and pine nuts."

Jamal did the slow headshake. "Oh man. Bondi. Oh man, oh man, oh man."

Bondi shrugged. "Whatever. Why, what did you get?"

Andrew looked embarrassed. "Nothing. Hamburger. Basic stuff, you know."

"Still the Paleo diet?" Jamal asked Bondi sympathetically.

Bondi grimaced. Andrew and Jamal exchanged glances and then silently pushed the french fries over to him.

"First things first, okay?" Jamal said, watching as Bondi scarfed down the fries. "Figure out your scholarship, buddy. Then we'll fix this Paleo thing."

Wilf

Wilf's mouth was still watering as Frank pulled up in front of Fat Johnnie's. Wilf had limited himself to just one hot dog each at Portillo's and the Wiener's Circle, even though it had practically killed him. But he wasn't messing around with this—he had to pace himself and take it seriously. According to his list, he still had at least seven hot dogs left to eat, and he didn't want to mess that up by overdoing it in the beginning. He'd dreamed of doing this for too long. Nothing was going to stop him from completing this quest. Nothing.

Frank stuck his head in Wilf's window.

"Still up for this?"

Wilf nodded. "Oh yeah."

. . . .

Melissa

Melissa slid into her seat just before the late bell rang and gave a little wave as Tanisha twisted around in her seat to look at her.

"So what happened? Did Masterson write you up? What did he want?" Tanisha whispered, keeping one eye on the science teacher, who was busy writing on the board.

Melissa snorted. "Just to accuse me of copying Tyler Blake's worksheet, that's all."

Tanisha made an exaggerated shocked face. "What the what? Doesn't he know Tyler's dumb as a rock?"

"Apparently not."

"Nobody's dumb enough to copy off Tyler!"

Melissa shrugged. "Nobody except Mr. Masterson, I guess."

Tanisha grinned. "What a doofus. What did you say?"

"I just messed with him a little. He really ticked me off." Melissa smirked. "So I said I wanted to get ice cream in 1910."

Tanisha sighed. "Yeah, you said it. I could totally go for that. I haven't done that in forever."

Melissa straightened up. "Wait, what?"

"What?" Tanisha jumped a little and stared at Melissa like she was freaking out. Which she pretty much was.

Melissa checked to make sure Mrs. Malone was still writing on the board and then thanked her lucky stars for long scientific formulas.

She tried to sound calm. "I said 'in 1910.'"

Tanisha eyed her suspiciously. "I know what you said."

"So what are you talking about?" Melissa's calm act wouldn't have convinced a chipmunk. Not that chipmunks are known for their body-language-reading skills.

Tanisha leaned back farther, like Melissa had gone rabid. "What are *you* talking about?"

"Nothing. I was just being stupid." Melissa resisted the urge to grab Tanisha's shoulders and shake her.

"Yeah, me too. I was just being stupid, too."

Melissa leaned forward more. "No, you weren't. You were talking about something real, weren't you?"

"No, I wasn't." Tanisha glared at her for a minute before finally sagging and lowering her voice. "Okay, I was, but don't tell anyone, okay? I know it's super lame."

"What? What's super lame?" Melissa sat on her hands. The urge to shake was back, and she knew that wouldn't go over well. Plus, a full-scale assault on Tanisha would definitely attract Mrs. Malone's attention.

"That ice cream parlor at the museum. You know, that old-timey street in the Museum of Science and Industry? It's supposed to be 1910." She looked around to make sure no one was listening. "Look, I know it's kid stuff, okay? I can't help that I still love it."

Melissa couldn't keep from grinning. "The museum has an ice cream parlor in 1910?"

Tanisha nodded warily. "Isn't that what you were talking about?"

Melissa started stuffing her books into her bag.

Tanisha watched with narrowed eyes. "What do you think you're doing?"

Melissa zipped up her book bag and smiled at Tanisha. She was going to play by her own rules now, and according to the new Melissa rules, she could invite friends to do things anytime she wanted. "Going to 1910 for ice cream. Want to come?"

Tanisha hesitated for only a second before she started stuffing her books into her backpack, too. "Oh man. Do I ever."

• •

Please excuse Melissa Burris and Tanisha Cole from school for the rest of the afternoon, as an educational opportunity regarding a possible scholarship has come up. They are both needed urgently, and their parents and guardians have fully agreed to this excursion, as you have verified over the phone.

Thank you,
Dimitri Omar
Representative of scholarship advisor
Mr. Butler, representative of Mr.
Smith, scholarship patron

Tanisha stood on the sidewalk eyeing Dimitri warily as he went into the elementary school. "And the note worked? Just like that?"

Melissa nodded. She didn't know how Dimitri had done it, but once she'd told him what they wanted to do, he'd gotten her grandmother to agree to everything over the phone. Then he did the same thing with Tanisha's parents. He'd had the office staff practically eating out of his hands. Even Mrs. Orlin had fluttered her eyelashes and said something sappy about his accent. If Melissa didn't know better, she'd say Dimitri was a hypnotist or something.

Tanisha still wasn't convinced. "But he's not my parent. I know they talked to my mom, but for real? They'll let us go just because?"

Melissa nodded again. "This scholarship thing is crazy."

Tanisha leaned in close. "I know you said you can't talk about it, but this can't be legit, Melissa. They've got to be working some angle here," she whispered. "You know that, right?"

Melissa made a face. "Believe me, I know. I can't figure out what that angle is, though."

Dimitri came out of the elementary school with Liam and Tanisha's little sister, Tabi, in tow.

Tanisha adjusted her backpack. "Well, whatever's going on, I'm not complaining. And thanks for saying Tabi could come, too. I couldn't exactly ditch her, since I'm supposed to watch her after school."

Melissa punched her lightly on the shoulder. "No problem. She'll keep Liam out of my hair, right?"

"Yeah, right," Tanisha said. "More like help him get *in* your hair."

Melissa snickered and then headed over to Dimitri. She shifted awkwardly as he opened the car door.

"Yeah, about that. Um, I think we're going to take the bus." She lowered her voice. "It would be mean for me and Liam to get a ride and make Tanisha and Tabi take the bus by themselves. And you know . . . the rules?"

Dimitri sighed heavily. "Melissa. You remember what I said? No breaking up sets?"

"Well, yeah."

"Sets come in all sizes." Dimitri held the car door open wider.

A grin spread over Melissa's face as she quickly turned and ushered Tanisha and Tabi into the car.

Wilf

Wilf's mouth had pretty much stopped watering by the time they pulled up in front of Superdawg. Fat Johnnie's had been awesome, and so had Jimmy's Red Hots, and whatever that place in between was. Wilf wasn't keeping track of the stops as well as he'd planned to. And, if he was going to be 100 percent honest, he was feeling a little full. Maybe even more than a little. The whole pacing-himself plan wasn't working quite as well as he'd hoped, either.

Frank hopped out of the car and stuck his head in Wilf's window. "Still up for this?" he asked. Frank had dropped out of the judging after Fat Johnnie's, proclaiming all of the hot dogs to be so excellent that he couldn't possibly choose which one was best. Unfortunately, Wilf felt the same way. He wasn't sure he was going to be able to crown a champion at the end of the day like he'd planned. And he sure as heck wasn't going to be up to trying each place a second time.

If he looked at it objectively, there wasn't a single part of his plan that was going like it was supposed to.

"Wilf?" Frank frowned. "We can stop anytime."

Wilf swallowed hard. He couldn't stop. This was a once-in-a-lifetime hot dog opportunity. "Nope, this is excellent. Ready to go."

· ·

Melissa

Melissa and Tanisha stared up at the ticket prices over the admission booth in the lobby of the Museum of Science and Industry. No wonder Gran never wanted to go to museums. Who knew they were so expensive? Melissa had worksheet money, but she'd spent some of it getting lunch. She didn't think what she had left would be enough.

She glanced over at Tanisha, who looked about as worried as Melissa felt.

Melissa's heart sank. The four of them coming here had been a bad idea. She felt around in her pocket, and her fingers folded around the debit card that had been in the packet. This was what it was for, right? And if she paid for Tanisha and Tabi and Liam, that would be okay, too, right? She wished the packet had been a little more clear about how closely they were going to be grilled on their expenses.

Melissa pulled out the debit card and held it in her closed fist. It seemed stupid not to use it. It would *have* to be okay. And if it wasn't, well, she'd just drum up a little extra homework money, that was all. Raid the computer fund if she had to. Not that there was all that much to raid.

Melissa had just taken a step toward the ticket counter when a strong pair of hands clamped on to her arms and moved her to the side.

"Excuse, please."

"Wha—?" Melissa gasped.

Dimitri Omar nodded at her as he went to the booth. "Five tickets, please. For me and my children."

Tanisha turned to Melissa, her eyes wide. "Who *is* this guy?"

Melissa grinned and slipped the debit card back into her pocket. "Does it matter? He's with us."

```
       FINNIGAN'S ICE CREAM PARLOR
 • • • • • • • • • • • • • • • • • • •

 1 large banana split
   chocolate and vanilla ice cream
   extra whipped cream

 1 large hot fudge sundae
   chocolate ice cream
   extra nuts, extra hot fudge,
   extra whipped cream, no cherry

 1 large hot fudge sundae
   mint chocolate chip ice cream
   extra hot fudge, extra whipped cream

 1 large banana split
   vanilla and strawberry ice cream
   extra whipped cream

 1 small vanilla ice cream cone
```

Liam wiped a smear of chocolate off of his cheek. "This ice cream is the best part."

Tanisha's sister, Tabi, shook her head, making the two puff ponytails on her head quiver like mouse ears. "That old-timey movie was the best part."

"Okay," Liam agreed. "But the ice cream is the best part *now*."

Tabi just nodded and took another bite of banana split. She was too busy eating to talk much.

Tanisha leaned back and surveyed Finnigan's Ice Cream Parlor. Aside from Dimitri Omar eating his ice cream cone near the front window, they were the only ones there. "So you know I won't rat you out, right? You can tell me what's going on here."

Melissa fiddled with her spoon. "I don't know. . . ."

"And if it's cheating you're worrying about, you can stop worrying. It's only cheating if I help your sorry butt." Tanisha grinned.

"Well, sorry, but you've already done that, Miss Ice-Cream-in-1910," Melissa said, rolling her eyes.

She stared down into her hot fudge. She'd already broken rule number three by telling Liam, so how much worse would it be to tell Tanisha, too? She kept thinking about the contract, though. Some of that language seemed pretty scary.

She looked at Tanisha apologetically and shook her head. "I'm sorry. I really can't. There was a contract. . . ."

Tanisha nodded. "Yeah, about that. Now, I'm not a lawyer—"

"No kidding."

"But I do know that you're way underage. I'm pretty sure

you can't legally sign a contract like that." Then she jerked her thumb at Liam. "Plus, you told this joker. So all bets are off."

Liam made a face.

Melissa glanced over at Dimitri. He nodded silently.

Melissa rolled her eyes again. It was a terrible idea. But somehow she couldn't imagine Tanisha selling her out. Or Dimitri, either, for that matter. "You win. Swear not to tell?"

Tanisha grinned. "Swear."

"I swear, too!" Tabi said, spraying a fine mist of banana.

"Me too!" Liam said. "Even though I already swore before."

"I also swear, even though I am already part of your team," Dimitri said from across the room.

Melissa groaned, but she couldn't help smiling. She was doomed. But at least she wasn't in this alone. And doomed or not, she couldn't remember the last time she'd had this much fun.

"So do you think this is it?" Tanisha asked after Melissa had filled her in on the details. "We take the picture here and you've solved the clue?"

Melissa shook her head. "There's that second part, about the newborns, see?"

She pushed the clue over to Tanisha.

Go to 1910 for ice cream, then stick around to watch the newborns.

Tanisha pored over the piece of paper and made a face. "Beats me, and I love this place. I don't remember seeing any babies. How'd you figure out the other clue?"

Melissa licked the last bit of hot fudge off of her spoon. "I figured out it was a trick, and once I knew that, I was able to find the statue. This last one was a fluke. I thought it was a joke, so I basically acted like a total crazy person, asking everyone I saw until someone knew what I was talking about. Thanks, by the way."

Tanisha waved it off. "No biggie. It got me ice cream, didn't it?"

"I doubt that would ever happen again, though." Melissa propped her chin on her hand. "I can't just go around asking people random questions and expecting it to work. But man, I wish it would."

"So go ahead and try it." Tanisha's eyes gleamed. "What could it hurt?"

Melissa crumpled her napkin and stood up. Crazy Person Act, commence. "Worth a shot, right?"

Tanisha put her hand over her mouth to keep from laughing as Melissa headed over to the woman at the cash register.

Melissa cleared her throat. "Um, excuse me. Could you tell me where I can find the newborns?" Melissa raised her eyebrows at Tanisha while she waited. This woman was going to think she was such a wack job.

The woman cocked her head to the side in the universal what-the-heck-are-you-talking-about? move. "Newborns?"

Melissa nodded. "Newborns. We'd like to see them."

The woman frowned. "I don't think I . . . OH! The newborns, right! Sure, they're on the other side of the building, with the genetics display."

Melissa felt like her heart had stopped. She looked back at Tanisha, who looked just as shocked. "Really? The genetics stuff?"

The woman smiled. "Yep, have fun!"

Melissa nodded again and walked back to the table in a daze. "The newborns are on the other side of the building."

"Near the genetics stuff."

"Right."

Tanisha pushed her bowl away. "Well, what are we waiting for? Let's go see some newborns."

• •

SPECULATION ON
WHAT THE NEWBORNS WILL BE

by Melissa Burris and Tanisha Cole

1. Not real babies. What kind of sick museum would keep a display of real babies? — Tanisha

2. Probably plastic babies that look all fake. And creepy. And will give me nightmares for years. Thanks, scholarship weirdos. —Melissa

3. Or maybe MUMMIFIED BABIES! OH MY GOSH, IT'S A MUSEUM— IT'S MUMMIFIED BABIES. WE'RE GOING TO SEE BABY MUMMIES! —Melissa

4. It's not that kind of museum. This is a science museum, not a mummy museum. So no mummified babies. (Probably.) —Tanisha

5. Fine, cloned babies, then. But if they're mummified babies, I'm out of here. —Melissa

Bondi

Bondi sat on a bench staring at the seal pool, his notebook dangling from one hand. He'd been to the bird house. He'd been to the bird of prey exhibit. He'd been to the swan pond. He'd been to the nature boardwalk. He'd even tried to feed some random ducks the remains of his lunch, but they didn't want anything to do with him or his chard. And none of the birds he'd seen had anything to do with his clue.

Someone sat down next to him, but Bondi didn't even bother to slide over to give them room. He didn't have the energy to be polite. He would probably never move again. What was the point? He was stumped.

Cigarette smoke drifted over from the other side of the bench. "So it's not here, I guess?"

Bondi shook his head. He'd recognize that raspy voice anywhere, even without the secondhand smoke.

"I can't figure it out. And if I don't figure it out, I won't win." Bondi's chest felt tight. He had to win. He always won. He was Bondi, winner kid. He didn't want to turn into regular Bondi, occasional loser. Who would care about a loser kid? But this wasn't the kind of thing where he could turn on the charm and come out on top. This was something that he had to do with brainpower alone. And his brain wasn't doing the job.

Inez crossed her arms and leaned back. "Kid, if there's one thing I'm sure of, it's this: you'll figure it out. I'm not saying it'll happen today. But you'll get it eventually. You just need to relax and give your brain a chance to work on it. You're putting too much pressure on yourself."

"Maybe," Bondi said, dragging his notebook across the pavement. "But the other kids—"

Inez gave a harsh barky laugh. "Who, that tall one? I don't think you need to worry about him just yet."

Bondi shot her a halfhearted smile.

"Listen, kid. I need you to be straight with me. You have to answer me something, okay?" Inez leaned forward and looked at him. "Okay?"

"Okay," Bondi said suspiciously, bracing himself for the worst.

"Good. Now, what the hell was that slop you were trying to foist off on those ducks? Man, oh man, I've never seen ducks run like that."

"That was chard. It's from the Paleo diet."

Inez snorted. "The Paleo what? Well, that explains a lot. All right, first things first. We've got to get some decent food in you. And then get a pretzel for you to give those ducks as an apology." She slapped Bondi on the knee. "Trust me. Once your stomach's full, you'll be thinking clearly and figuring out clues all over the place."

Bondi gave a weak laugh and stood up. "Sounds good." Maybe Inez was right. Food was the answer. And he didn't care what he ate, as long as it wasn't green or leafy.

. . . .

Bondi: Please, Mom. No more chard.

Dad: Seconded.

Mom: Where's your sense of adventure? Fine. No more chard. What are your feelings about radicchio?

Wilf

Wilf stared at the blade of grass a few inches from his nose. He would never eat another hot dog as long as he lived. He didn't even want to think about how many he'd had. Even thinking the words *hot dog* made him want to puke.

"You okay down there?" Frank said. It sounded like he was a million miles away.

Wilf made a gurgling noise.

"Okay, just let me know when you're done."

Wilf could hear Frank walking back toward the car. Wilf wasn't sure where they were exactly. The grass was nice, though. Nice and long. Probably didn't get cut very often, but that was okay by Wilf. It tickled his nose a little, but that was okay, too. He liked the way the grass smelled.

Wilf closed his eyes and tried to think about anything but hot dogs and his stomach, and the way Frank had been hitting the brakes a little too hard ever since that last place. It could've been Wilf's imagination. But whatever it was, it totally did Wilf's stomach in. Yeah, probably Frank's driving, Wilf decided. Not the hot dogs.

"Thanks . . . needed to report . . ."

Wilf could just make out a voice over the sound of cars whizzing past. It sounded like Frank, but who was around for Frank to talk to? Oh man, Wilf hoped he didn't end up in a hilarious puking video online. Not much he could do to stop it, though, since he couldn't seem to move at the moment.

"Yeah, that's what I thought. But he thinks it's solved."

Frank's voice was so faint that Wilf could barely hear him. Frank was probably talking on the phone, Wilf decided. That made sense. But then he heard a low, rumbling voice answer back.

Wilf strained to hear what the other person was saying, but the traffic drowned it out. He briefly considered standing up, but when he shifted his weight, his stomach immediately voiced its disapproval. Wilf flopped back down. It probably didn't matter who Frank was talking to, anyway.

"Really? . . . not quite fair . . . if you say so," Wilf heard Frank say. "Right . . . bigger picture. Sure."

The other voice said something in response, but Wilf's ears weren't up to the job.

Wilf opened his eyes. A tiny green inchworm was walking on a blade of grass up near his forehead.

" . . . if that's what you want me to do . . ." Frank said.

Wilf heard a car door slam. The inchworm reared up and waved its tiny legs around.

Wilf smiled at it. "Don't worry, inchworm," Wilf said. "I promise not to puke on you."

The inchworm looked doubtful. Wilf didn't blame it.

• •

Melissa

Melissa stood over the incubator smiling in satisfaction. "Newborns."

Tanisha peered over her shoulder. "Yep. And some not-quite-yet-borns."

The incubator in the center of the room was filled with eggs, hatching eggs, and chicks that had just managed to escape their eggs. The older chicks ran around looking all fluffy and cute, rubbing their adorableness in the faces of the just-born ones, who didn't have the energy to do anything but lie on the ground looking slimy and wet. Melissa snapped a photo of the slimiest chick. She had a soft spot for the disgusting ones.

"Can't get much newer than that guy," Melissa said, snapping another photo. That guy was the poster chick for newborns. The fluffy chicks crowded around, like they were trying to get in the picture, too, but Melissa pointedly ignored them.

"Unless you count that one," Liam said, pointing at a beak poking out of an egg. "He's newer than your gross guy."

Melissa took one last photo and slipped the camera back in her book bag. "No dice, buddy," she said to Liam. "One measly beak doesn't qualify him as born."

Liam made a face. "Yeah, I guess. Sorry, dude," he said to the beak. The beak ignored him.

Tanisha watched as Melissa stowed the camera away. "So you've got a photo of the ice cream shop, and a photo of that guy. Is that it for the clue?"

Melissa nodded. "I think so. That means I've got two out of three. I may have a real shot at winning this."

"That's great. I mean it, really great. But"—Tanisha bit her lip—"does that mean we have to go now?"

"You want to still hang out?" Melissa said in surprise.

"Not if you don't want to. I mean, I get that you're busy."

Melissa punched her lightly on the arm. "*I'm* busy? You're the one who's always got something going on!"

"Me? Yeah, right!" Tanisha punched her back. "No seriously, this was cool. I'm glad we finally got to hang out outside of school."

Melissa grinned. "Me too."

"But what about . . . ?" Tanisha jerked her head in Dimitri's direction and lowered her voice. "He okay with us staying longer?"

Melissa looked over at Dimitri, who was peering at a not-quite-born chick valiantly working to get a foot out of his shell. "Dimitri?" she said hesitantly.

He waved her off. "Melissa, do not disturb me. I am watching our little friend."

"You are?"

"Yes. And most likely will be until closing time. That will be sufficient time, no?" He took his eyes off of the chick long enough to raise an eyebrow at her.

Melissa and Tanisha gave each other a discreet low five. "Sure, no problem. That sounds like a terrific plan!" Melissa said. "That guy needs your support."

"Right!" Tanisha beamed. "Don't let us get in your way. We wouldn't want to mess up your plans."

"Thank you." Dimitri's mouth curled into the faintest smile. "I appreciate your understanding."

"Submarine!" Tabi cheered under her breath, grabbing Liam by the arm and heading off toward the elevator.

"No, coal mine!" Liam said, trying to pull Tabi in the opposite direction.

"Both!" Melissa said, herding them up as Tanisha consulted her map.

Dimitri's smile got wider. He watched the chick waggle his foot as the kids disappeared down the steps.

SOLUTIONS TO CLUES

By: _Melissa Burris_

1. Go to the site of Lorado Taft's Death in 1909.

SOLUTION: ~~Up yours.~~ Eternal Silence statue by Lorado Taft in Graceland Cemetery.

2. Go to 1910 for ice cream, then stick around to watch the newborns.

SOLUTION: Museum of Science and Industry, Finnigan's Ice Cream Parlor on Yesterday's Main Street, followed by the hatching chicks. Ice cream was eaten, and chicks were observed.

3.

Wilf

Wilf smushed his face up against the cool window of the car, trying not to move his head too much. He'd left a neat little pile of partially digested hot dogs by the side of the road a few miles back, but he still had vast reserves ready and waiting to aim and fire. Wilf didn't like to think about how easy it would be for him to go off again.

"Hey, kid, need to make a pit stop, okay?" Frank called from the front seat as he pulled the car over.

"No, I'm okay," Wilf croaked. "I don't need to stop."

Stopping would be bad. If he thought about why he might need to stop, he'd need to stop. Too late—he needed to stop.

"No, this stop's for me," Frank said before Wilf could open his mouth to try to say anything. "Just a little Frank time." He got out of the car and opened Wilf's door. Wilf tumbled out, catching himself in time to stagger back against the car in what he hoped was a cool, I'm-not-going-to-puke pose.

Frank took a deep breath and clapped Wilf on the shoulder. "So, Wilf."

Wilf recovered from the unexpected shoulder clap, but barely. He glared up at Frank. He didn't know what the heck was wrong with that guy, but he was acting like a total weirdo.

Frank took another deep breath and looked around. Then he raised his eyebrows at Wilf significantly. "So, Wilf."

Wilf blinked and leaned against the car again. He hoped he wasn't getting car dirt all over his back, but he probably was. It would look great with the side-of-the-road dirt all over his front, and the flopping-down-in-the-grass stains on his jeans.

Frank raised his eyebrows again and then seemed to sag. "So what a view, huh?" He sounded falsely chipper, like he was in a commercial or something.

Wilf glanced around. They were downtown, on Michigan or Congress somewhere. It looked like downtown, anyway. "Yeah, I guess. Are you allowed to just stop here?"

Frank sighed. "Probably not. But just take a look, Wilf. What a skyline. And check out those statues. Have you ever seen anything like that before? Just take a look at that. Pretty inspiring statues, right?"

Wilf peered up through his bangs at the statues looming above them to the left and right. The two Native American warriors on horses stood on either side of the road, their arms outstretched in menacing poses. It looked like they might be naked, too, but Wilf wasn't planning to investigate that. Frank smiled at him expectantly. Wilf nodded. Cool statues. He'd seen them before.

"Yeah, they're great."

"Great," Frank muttered.

"Yeah. Great."

A cab driver leaned on his horn, cussing at them as he cut around their car. Frank ignored him.

Frank squinted up at the statues again. "So, Wilf," he said, sounding strange and stiff and weirdly defeated, "you know what I like best about these guys? Their weapons. Cool, right?"

Wilf stared at Frank like he had gone completely insane. He blew on his bangs and then threw his head back to examine the statues. "They don't have any weapons, Frank."

"Exactly." Frank turned to Wilf and stared him straight in the eye. It creeped Wilf out a little, to be honest.

"Exactly?"

"Exactly." Frank cleared his throat. "Like their weapons were . . ." He hesitated and looked away, his face getting red. "Like they were broken. They're called the *Bowman* and the *Spearman*, you know. The statues, I mean."

"*Bowman* and *Spearman*. Huh. And the weapons are . . ." Wilf trailed off. His eyes got wide. He grabbed Frank by the shoulders.

"Oh man, Frank, you know what? You know what?"

Frank turned back. "What?"

"I think these guys are—wait . . ." Wilf grabbed his backpack out of the car and rummaged around until he'd found his clue packet. "Look—*Bowman* and *Spearman*, see?" He read from his notebook. "He breaks the bow and shatters the spear! That's these guys! This is the solution to the clue! It's not just the Bible verse, it's talking about them!"

Frank's smile was strained. "Really? That's amazing, Wilf! Congratulations!"

Wilf grinned. "Here, I've got to take a picture!" He shoved his backpack into Frank's arms as he fumbled for the camera. He couldn't believe how awesome he was. He was rocking this whole clue thing.

After he'd taken a bunch of photos from different angles, Frank opened the car door again. "I think you're covered, kid. Now, let's get you home before the cops give me a ticket."

Wilf nodded and piled into the car. He didn't even feel like he was going to barf anymore. Well, maybe he did, but not every second, like before. He put the camera back into his backpack as Frank pulled out into traffic.

Frank didn't say much on the way back to Wilf's apartment, but that was fine. Wilf had a ton of things to think about. Because one thing was certain: Wilf was back on top.

SOLUTIONS TO CLUES

By: WILF SAMSON

1. Jeremiah 6:23 plus Psalm 46:9

SOLUTION: ~~JEREMIAH 6:23 AND PSALM 46:9. THEY'RE IN THE BIBLE. (ANY BIBLE PROBABLY WORKS, BUT DEFINITELY IN THE NEW INTERNATIONAL VERSION.)~~ BOWMAN AND SPEARMAN STATUES ON CONGRESS PLAZA IN DOWNTOWN CHICAGO.

2.

3.

To: Butler
From: Frank Jennings
Subject: Not what I signed up for

Butler:
Once again, I want to register my protest. This is not the way things were supposed to go. I was hired as a driver and a chaperone, and today's request went way over the line. I don't want to be forced into that position again.

Sincerely,
Frank

To: Frank Jennings
From: Butler
Subject: RE: Not what I signed up for

Frank:
Noted. Your assignments are not without purpose. I sincerely hope you understand this and will continue to act according to our requests. You know what's at stake. Remember the big picture. Don't let us down.
Butler

Bondi

Bondi smoothed the cover of his notebook carefully as he slipped it inside his messenger bag. As tempting as it was, he would not open it. Not even a peek. He wasn't going to think about the stupid scholarship at all. No birds, no clocks, no nothing. Bondi's tried-and-true research-his-butt off method of investigation hadn't panned out, so he was going to try Inez's totally-ignore-the-problem-and-the-solution-will-magically-appear method. It was worth a shot, at least.

Bondi headed into the living room, where his mom was sitting with her feet up on the coffee table. The TV was off, and she seemed to be watching his dad fiddle with a bunch of cords.

"Homework done already?" she said, taking a sip of iced tea as Bondi's dad cursed softly behind the TV cabinet.

"All done," Bondi said, smiling.

"Of course it is—our kid's the best at everything!"

Bondi's dad said from behind the cabinet. "Isn't that right, Bondi?"

"Right," Bondi said, his smile fading a bit as he sat down on the couch. Inez's plan had to work. He couldn't let them down. "So what's going on?"

His mom chuckled softly. "The wireless is all messed up again, and we're trying to fix it. Your dad's show is on in a little bit."

"We're never going to make it in time!" Bondi's dad said from behind the TV cabinet. "I'm never going to get this fixed."

He popped his head up and looked at them. "You watching with us tonight, Bondi? I don't know if . . ." He glanced at his wife.

"Yeah, that show is a little violent. We can save it for later. Want to pick a movie instead?" Bondi's mom patted him on the leg. "Assuming we can get the DVD player to work, that is."

"What, did I mess up the DVD player now?" His dad groaned and flopped back onto the carpet. "What did I unplug that I shouldn't have?"

Bondi's mom snickered and winked at Bondi.

Bondi leaned back into the couch. Watching a movie was pretty much the furthest you could get from researching clues. It sounded like that would fit right in with his new Inez problem-solving strategy. "My pick?"

His mom poked him in the ribs and gave him a serious look. "Well, I don't know. Are you picking something with robots and explosions?"

Bondi grinned. "Of course."

His mom handed him the remote. "Done."

Wilf

Wilf lay in his bed waiting for his mom to get home from her night out. He'd been planning to tell her about how he'd figured out the clue. But the more he thought about it and what he would say, the more it seemed wrong, somehow.

Frank had acted so weird earlier. Wilf knew it was crazy, but it was almost like Frank had deliberately pointed him to the solution. But that didn't make any sense. Why would Frank do that?

And how would he even know?

A car door slammed downstairs. Wilf scrambled over to the window, but it wasn't his mom—it was just that guy from the second floor with the neurotic dog that peed whenever you looked at it.

Wilf lay back down. Frank didn't even know what the clues *were*, right? There was no way he could give Wilf hints, let alone point him toward a solution. Besides, that would be cheating. Wouldn't it?

Wilf groaned. He'd tried to tell his dad about the whole thing when he'd called earlier that night, just to see what he thought of the situation. But it all came out wrong, and his dad couldn't talk long, anyway. He didn't seem that interested in hearing about the different kinds of hot dogs, and Wilf hadn't even wanted to get into the puking.

Besides, it was hard to keep straight exactly how things had happened. That whole puking thing had made the rest of the day kind of hard to remember. Especially that part with the inchworm. Wilf frowned. Had that even happened? It was weird to think that he'd hung out with an inchworm. And had Frank really been talking to someone? That seemed weird, too.

Another car door slammed downstairs, and Wilf jumped for the window. His mom was just coming inside.

Wilf pulled on his bathrobe and hurried into the hallway.

He was being an idiot. It had been a lucky coincidence, that's all. And Frank had probably just been watching some show on his phone or something. Being alone was making Wilf paranoid. And being paranoid was the last thing he wanted to be.

Wednesday

Melissa's Clues:

Go to the site of Lorado Taft's Death in 1909.

Freeze! Look to the building where Tarzan swam to find your "Contribution."

Go to 1910 for ice cream, then stick around to watch the newborns.

Bondi's Clues:

Eli should've called this bubbler "Spitty Geese with Fish Huggers."

Help your bird friends get Wright to the Root of the matter as you spiral down from 12 to 2.

Surrounded by glass, you'll find the world at your feet.

Wilf's Clues:

Jeremiah 6:23 plus Psalm 46:9

Madame Tussaud and Mrs. O'Leary would be proud of their little blue friend.

???

Bondi

Bondi was poring over his notebooks, his feet propped on the chair across from him, when Jamal knocked his legs down.

"Hey!" Bondi said, sitting up.

Jamal smirked as he slid into the now empty chair. "Man, you're still at this scholarship stuff? You haven't solved it *yet*?"

Bondi shrugged. "I'm almost there."

"And you still can't talk about it?"

Bondi shrugged again.

"You're losing your touch." Jamal shook his head sadly and then reached out and snatched the notebook away from Bondi. "Let me see. Ol' Jamal can figure this out for you." He peered down at the page.

"Ol' Jamal?"

"That's right," Jamal said, examining the clue.

Bondi folded his arms. "You're not supposed to help me."

"I'm not helping, I'm just reading," Jamal said.

"Solved it yet?" Bondi said when Jamal finally handed it back.

"Yeah, right." Jamal snorted. "That's messed up, man. Beats me what that's about."

Bondi slumped back in his chair. "Yeah, it's tricky. I can't figure it out."

"Yeah, it's crazy." Jamal tapped the paper. "I mean, why are those words capitalized, for one thing?"

Bondi stared at him. "What do you mean?"

Jamal pointed at the clue. "Those capitalized words. How come they're special? Are they names, or what? Or is your clue man just lousy at grammar?"

Bondi peered at the clue again.

Help your bird friends get Wright to the Root of the matter as you spiral down from 12 to 2.

"Oh man!" His eyes were wide. "Dang, Jamal! Names!" He scrambled up and hurried over to an empty computer terminal. "This has *got* to be it."

He typed *Root* and *Wright* into the search engine and held his breath as he hit ENTER. Jamal looked over his shoulder. "Hold up, TheRoot.com? That's an online magazine."

Bondi waved him off. "Yeah, but that's not it. I'm not being specific enough."

Jamal pointed at the keyboard. "Type in *bird*, too."

Bondi's eyes gleamed. "Not just bird . . ."

He typed in *Root Wright bird* and *Chicago*. Then he hit ENTER.

Jamal punched him on the shoulder when the results came up. "Way to go, man!"

Bondi grinned and clicked on the second link. He had it now.

The Rookery, Chicago, IL

Designed by the famed architectural team of Daniel H. Burnham and John W. Root, with a lobby redesigned by Frank Lloyd Wright, the Rookery is one of the most historically significant buildings in Chicago. Originally completed in 1888, the building

"Inez. Inez. Pick up. Pick up, Inez." Bondi crouched in the library stacks, chanting into his phone. His original plan had been to call Inez, ditch school, and get to the Rookery, but since Inez wasn't answering, he didn't know what to do, except keep calling or start walking. He sure didn't want to wait until school was over, he knew that much.

"This is Inez. You know what to do." Even in her message she sounded like she was smoking.

Bondi waited until the voice mail beeped. "Inez, it's Bondi. I figured it out. Pick me up, and I'll tell you where we need to go. Call me back. Bye."

Bondi hung up and then sat staring at the phone like he expected Inez to magically appear on the screen. She didn't.

Bondi hit REDIAL just as a shadow blocked out the light above him.

"Having fun, Mr. Johnson?" Mrs. Marlowe, the librarian, was frowning down at him, arms folded. She didn't look like she was going to buy any explanations about solving clues and competitions.

Bondi smiled up at her, trying not to stare at her tapping foot. Mrs. Marlowe's feet were always puffed up, like giant marshmallows that she'd stuffed into shoes two sizes too small. It wasn't a good look. "I believe your class period has started. Were you intending to join them?"

Bondi slid his phone into his pocket. Mrs. Marlowe wasn't someone to mess with, not with feet like that. Feet like that make you crabby.

"You know, I was, but these books, they all look so interesting! I was having such a hard time deciding between them that I must've lost track of time. Could you recommend something? Please?"

Mrs. Marlowe crouched down and looked at the shelf.

"Oh, well, certainly. You're interested in mythology, I see." She tapped her finger to her lips thoughtfully and then pulled out a book. "I'd recommend this Edith Hamilton as a starting point. Now, run and check it out and get to class, young man," she said in a mock-stern voice.

"Yes, ma'am." Bondi grinned as he took the book and hurried to the checkout desk.

He turned the cell phone ringer to vibrate as he turned the corner. As soon as Inez called him back, he'd be on his way to collecting his prize. And no puffy-footed librarian would be able to stop him.

Frank ran the buffer cloth over the hood of the car and eyed the cell phone on the table. It had been ringing nonstop for the past ten minutes. He'd considered answering it, but then decided against it. He had a good idea who was calling.

Inez strolled into the garage carrying a box of doughnuts and a bag of fruit from the grocery on the corner. Nodding at Frank, she chucked the doughnuts onto the table, then pulled out a chair with one foot and plunked down in the seat in one fluid motion.

"So," she said, watching Frank buff the car, "what'd I miss?"

Frank jerked his head in the direction of the phone. "Looks like somebody tried to call you."

Inez pulled the phone over and looked at the screen. "Seventeen missed calls? What the—?"

Frank shrugged and kept buffing.

Inez called up her voice mail and listened, a smile spreading across her face. She hung up after message number four and hit the first number on her speed dial.

She grinned at Frank while it rang. "You know what's going on?"

Frank sighed. "I've got an idea."

"You've got an idea." She snickered. Then she smiled into the phone. "Butler. Inez. It's on. He's done it, so get ready."

She slammed the phone onto the table and smirked at Frank. "Things are about to get a lot more interesting."

Bondi was waiting out front when Inez pulled up. "Where *were* you? Did you lose your phone or something?" he demanded, hopping into the backseat of the car before Inez even had a chance to stop completely.

"Hold your horses, kiddo. Now where do you need to get so badly?"

"The Rookery—it's a building on LaSalle." Bondi leaned forward between the seats so he was practically in the front seat. "It's the third solution—one last picture and I'll win the whole thing!"

"Rookery, got it. I know the one." Inez nodded, shooting a smile at Bondi. "What did I tell you? I knew you'd get it! You just had to have a little faith in yourself! Now, buckle up and hang on."

Inez hit the gas so hard she almost sideswiped a city bus. The bus driver leaned on the horn, but Inez just laughed. "I'll get you there, kid!"

Bondi scrambled to get his seat belt fastened. "Just make sure it's in one piece!"

Wilf

Frank cracked a smile as Wilf piled into the car after school, but his smile didn't seem to go all the way up to his eyes. Wilf wished he hadn't puked quite so much the day before. He didn't want Frank thinking of him as the pukey kid or worrying about his backseat.

"So, um, sorry about yesterday. We okay?" Wilf said in a rush. He figured he had to say something right away so it wouldn't be weird. Or weirder.

Frank smiled, and it seemed like a real one this time. "No problem, boss. I don't know how you put away that many hot dogs. It was pretty impressive. I sure couldn't have done it!"

Wilf grinned. "Yeah, I guess." He fiddled with the envelope of clues in his lap. He hadn't looked at it since he'd figured out that last one. He wasn't even sure he still had all the clues in there.

It wasn't like he'd even planned on solving any of the clues in the first place. Why bother when there was zero chance he'd win the contest? He was just out to have fun while it lasted. But he hated feeling like he was disappointing Frank. And for some reason, Frank seemed to have a thing about figuring out the clues.

He'd have to get them organized if he was going to finish solving them. But there was probably plenty of time for that, right? It's not like there was any huge rush. He was pretty sure Miss Apple Shampoo wasn't out there solving many clues.

Frank stopped at the light and adjusted the radio. "So what's up for today? There are still some things on that list of yours. Zoo? Boat trip? I'm vetoing skydiving."

Wilf kept looking at the envelope. "Zoo sounds good to me." He cleared his throat. "Hey, Frank?"

Frank looked at him in the rearview mirror. "Yeah?"

"That *Bowman* and *Spearman* stuff. You didn't know that was the answer to the clue, did you? I mean, that was all a coincidence, right?"

Frank looked away and fiddled with the glove compartment. He didn't seem to be getting anything out, though. "What? Are you kidding? How would I know the answer to your clue?"

Wilf relaxed. "I know, right? How would you know?"

"Right. How would I?" Frank nodded. "So Lincoln Park Zoo sound okay?"

"Sure," Wilf said, cracking his window. "Sounds great."

TENTATIVE SCHEDULE, WILF SAMSON: (UPDATED)

~~1. Go to aquarium.~~

~~2. Visit Sears Tower Skydeck Ledge (Willis Tower, whatever).~~

3. Watch laser light show at the planetarium.

~~4. Go to zoo (both Lincoln Park and Brookfield, if possible).~~

~~5. Ride Ferris wheel at Navy Pier.~~

6. Seadog boat ride.

~~7. Hot Dog taste-test-a-thon. Fat Johnnie's vs. Wiener's Circle vs. Jimmy's Red Hots vs. Superdawg vs. others to be named later (until puking commences)~~ PUKING COMPLETE.

8. Get psychic reading.

ALSO: FIGURE OUT CLUES AND SOLUTIONS.
~~9. GO SKYDIVING.~~ Vetoed by Frank.
10. TAKE HELICOPTER TOUR.
11. KAYAK ON CHICAGO RIVER.
12. PLAY BUBBLE SOCCER (FIRST, FIGURE OUT WHAT
    EXACTLY BUBBLE SOCCER IS.)

Melissa

Melissa plunked her head down on the library table, groaning as she pushed the papers away. She'd had a whole afternoon to herself, with Liam at his friend's house, and she'd wasted it. She was never going to figure out the last clue. It was hopeless. She'd read it a million times, and if she read it a million times more, it would never be any clearer. Never. She mouthed the words silently, hoping she didn't look like a crazy person.

*Freeze! Look to the building
where Tarzan swam to find your
"Contribution."*

It seemed pretty obvious that Tarzan was the key there, so that seemed like an obvious starting point. Big mistake. It wasn't that she couldn't find enough information about Tarzan. She was finding way too much. She'd looked up Tarzan, the character. She'd looked up Edgar Rice Burroughs, the author of Tarzan. She'd looked up Johnny Weissmuller and Christopher Lambert and a gazillion other actors who had played Tarzan. Practically all of them had some connection to Chicago. It was hopeless.

"Melissa?"

She turned her head to the side so that her cheek pressed flat against the cool table. That was all she was willing to do. Actually lifting her head was beyond her at this point. "What?"

Tanisha crouched down and tilted her head sideways to look at her. "Problem?"

Melissa groaned and turned her head back, smushing her nose into the table. "I'll never get it," she muttered sadly.

"Well, let me see."

Melissa heard the papers she had scattered across the table start rustling.

"Nooo—" Melissa started, but Tanisha cut her off.

"Relax, I've got my English notebook in front so it doesn't look like I'm helping. Smith's spies will never know."

Melissa didn't even have the energy to protest.

"Hmph," Tanisha said finally. She picked up a hunk of hair hanging over Melissa's face and peered into her eyes. "What's the problem? Looks straightforward enough."

Melissa snorted in disgust and lifted her head, pushing the hair out of her face. "Oh sure. Edgar Rice Burroughs was from Chicago. Probably went swimming all over. Johnny Weissmuller was a freaking Olympic swimmer. Swimmers *swim*, Tanisha. He swam at the YMCA, the InterContinental Hotel, someplace called the Medinah Athletic Club, and Fullerton Beach. Heck, probably *all* the beaches, plus a gazillion other places. I haven't even gotten into the thousand other people who played Tarzan and where they swam. Did you know that Disney made sequels to that animated Tarzan movie that went straight to video? Heck, *Gonzo* from the Muppets played Tarzan in a TV special. *It's too much Tarzan!*"

Melissa knew she sounded crazy, but crazy was the only way she knew how to be right then.

Tanisha rolled her eyes and pulled out the chair next to Melissa. "Well, you can rule out the beach because this clue says *building*. I say we look up those buildings you listed and see which one has some kind of 'contribution.' It's in quotes, Melissa; it's got to be a thing. Okay? Sooner we start, the sooner it's done. Tabi's got ballet at the Y today, so I'm all yours."

Melissa sniffed and gave a weird hiccup-y sob. Then she nodded. Even if they didn't figure it out, at least she wasn't doing it alone. Tanisha would help her. Tanisha, her first real friend in forever. That was the one good thing to come out of this whole stupid contest. She'd have company in the insane asylum. And she knew one thing for sure: she was never watching anything Tarzan ever again.

• •

Bondi

Bondi stood in the entryway of the Rookery Building, slowly turning as he took it all in. It was a pretty amazing place. The floor was a slick, patterned mosaic of tiles, and a wide marble stairway led up to the second floor. Gilding and elaborate metalwork lined all the walls, and an intricate iron stairway rose up from the second floor. The ceiling was latticed glass, with exposed white iron rafters.

"Whoa," Bondi breathed, looking around. It was too bad he was in such a rush. But he had to find the clock—then he'd be done. He could come back for a tour of this place after he'd snagged that scholarship.

He sauntered up to a woman at the information desk. "Excuse me, ma'am?"

She blinked expectantly at him.

"This building, does it have a famous clock somewhere? I'm interested in architecture."

The woman furrowed her brow, made a thinking face, and then shook her head. "No, I'm sorry. I don't know of any famous clock here. The Rookery is really more famous for the light court and its staircase. See all that natural light coming in? That's why this is called the light court. Amazing, isn't it?"

Bondi nodded. It wasn't like he was going to argue. It was a pretty awesome place. Just pretty disappointing from a clue standpoint.

"And if you're interested in architecture, you should really check out the stairway."

Bondi pointed politely to the marble stairs leading to the second floor. "That one?" Like he cared about the staircase. If it wasn't a clock, he wasn't interested.

The woman shook her head. "No, see the iron one, on

the next floor? That's the Oriel staircase designed by John Root. It goes from the second floor right up to the top."

Bondi's breath caught in his throat. "Let me guess. To the twelfth floor? Twelve down to two?"

The woman smiled. "That's right."

Bondi grinned. "Oh yeah, can't miss that!" He waved a quick good-bye as he hurried across the light court to the stairs, his camera already out of his pocket.

"Oriel staircase, here I come."

Melissa

Melissa looked up from her notes, clutching her note-book so tightly her knuckles were white. Tanisha had been enthusiastic at first, but now she was slumped over the arm of her chair, flipping through a book like each turn of the page was physically painful.

"Tanisha," Melissa said, her voice cracking, "what hotel did I say Johnny Weissmuller swam in?"

She bit her lip while Tanisha heaved herself upright and grabbed a notebook from under a pile on the table.

She flipped it open. "It says here . . . the InterContinental. Why?"

Melissa squeezed her notebook tighter. "And I said Medinah Athletic Club, too, right?"

Tanisha nodded. "So?"

"So according to this, they're the same place."

Tanisha's eyes gleamed. "For real?"

"For real."

Tanisha threw the notebook down onto the table. "Well, shoot, we've got to find out about that building!"

• •

Bondi

Inez snapped her phone shut and slapped Bondi on the back. "Good work, kid. Now here's what we do. You get prints of those photos made, and then we have a meeting with the big boss, Mr. Smith. I don't want to jinx things, but it looks like you've done it."

Bondi didn't answer. He was already halfway down the block to the drugstore.

Melissa

Melissa and Tanisha burst out of the building with such force that the door smacked into the brick wall and bounced back. It would've hit Melissa in the face if she and Tanisha hadn't already leaped down the steps and made it to the sidewalk by the time it whacked back into place.

"Dimitri!" Melissa yelled, out of breath. "We did it! It's the InterContinental Hotel!"

Dimitri frowned. "What's the InterContinental Hotel?"

"Medinah Athletic Club!" Tanisha said, leaning over and pressing the stitch in her side. They'd raced the entire length of the school to get to where Dimitri was parked.

"They're the *same building*," Melissa said.

"And that's where Johnny Weissmuller used to swim, in the pool there," Tanisha said.

"And he was Tarzan," Melissa explained, bobbing on the

balls of her feet as Dimitri looked from her to Tanisha like he was watching a Ping-Pong game.

"And that's what the clue said: *Tarzan*. And that part where it says *freeze*? At the beginning?"

"The InterContinental Hotel has these three friezes on its sides, way up, a couple of stories up." Melissa frowned. "How many?"

Tanisha rolled her eyes. "I don't remember. But a lot. Eight, maybe?"

"I thought twelve."

"Whatever. But anyway, Dimitri, the friezes have names."

"And one of them is called Contribution!" Melissa finished, folding her arms and looking at Dimitri triumphantly. He blinked at her with a mournful expression on his face.

Melissa didn't like that expression. She unzipped her book bag to get the clue out. Maybe if he read it. "See, the clue says—"

"Melissa," Dimitri said softly.

She really didn't like that tone. "What?"

"The boy, Bondi. He solved his third clue."

Melissa went cold. She glanced at Tanisha and then quickly turned away. Tanisha looked like she was going to barf, and Melissa knew she probably looked worse. She sure felt worse, like she'd been smacked in the face. She swallowed hard. "So what does that mean? Is he the winner? Am I too late?"

Dimitri gave a helpless shrug. "Is not for me to say. But his meeting with Mr. Smith"—he consulted his watch—"is now."

· ·

Bondi

Bondi stood in front of the desk, trying to hang loose while Mr. Smith stared at him, his eyes narrowed and his fingers steepled. Bondi wasn't going to let this Smith guy get under his skin, though, not when he was about to be crowned the big winner.

Mr. Smith finally sniffed. "Butler tells me you think you have figured out the clues."

Bondi nodded. "That's right. I know I did. I solved them and took the pictures, just like you wanted."

Mr. Smith nodded. "So you say. We shall see. Now." He pulled out the first slip of paper and started to read: "*Eli* should've called this bubbler 'Spitty Geese with Fish Huggers.' And the solution?"

Bondi grinned. "Buckingham Fountain, most famous fountain in Chicago."

Mr. Smith nodded and put the paper down. He picked up the second slip and read: *"Help your bird friends get Wright to the Root of the matter as you spiral down from twelve to two."*

"It's the Rookery Building on South LaSalle. The *bird friends* part is referring to the name of the building, and the Oriel staircase there is famous—it goes from the second floor to the twelfth. Wright and Root designed the building and the lobby."

Mr. Smith nodded again. "Good. And finally, *Surrounded by glass, you'll find the world at your feet?"*

"The Skydeck Ledge at the Sears—sorry—Willis Tower."

Mr. Smith nodded, his eyes gleaming. "Very good. Very good indeed."

Bondi's grin widened, and he felt the tension melting away. He didn't know why he'd been so worried about losing. "So I got them right?"

"Yes, yes, good work. Very good. And you have photos?" Mr. Smith held out his hand.

Bondi stepped forward and handed him the photos,

smiling a little at the one of him lying on the floor of the Skydeck. Sure, it was a little silly, but silly never hurt anybody. Besides, it wasn't like Mr. Smith would care.

But Mr. Smith frowned and his face turned three shades darker. "What is the meaning of this? Why are you in these photos?"

Bondi shrugged in what he hoped was an unconcerned way. But to be honest, he was getting a little concerned. "You didn't say we shouldn't be in the pictures. And I thought you'd want evidence that I was there."

Mr. Smith bristled. "I do not care if *you* were there." He

threw the photos at Bondi. "Not acceptable. Get me new photos, or you forfeit the game."

"But . . . what? *Forfeit?* Are you serious?"

"Redo the photos or be disqualified. One of the other children will be declared the winner." The gleam in Mr. Smith's eyes had taken on a tinge of crazy.

Bondi gathered the photos from the floor and stared down at them. Every muscle in his body wanted to fling them back at Mr. Smith, but . . . forfeit. He couldn't forfeit. Not when he should be the winner. He clenched his jaw instead. "But . . . fine. Okay, fine. I'll be back."

Bondi took the camera that Butler handed him and hurried out of the office without a backwards glance.

"Ridiculous so-and-so, thinking he's all that," Bondi muttered under his breath. While he waited for the elevator, he squatted down and shuffled through the other photos in the drugstore envelope. By the time he'd gotten through half of them, he'd started to feel better. It wasn't quite that bad. He'd gotten one shot of the Skydeck by itself. Sure, it was a picture he'd taken by mistake when he was pulling the camera out of his pocket, but it counted. And there was a shot he'd taken on the staircase at the Rookery—except for what looked like the tip of his thumb, you couldn't see him at all.

It was really just the fountain that was the problem. He

was in every single one of those photos, grinning like an idiot.

Bondi saved the two good shots in the envelope and stuffed the rest into his messenger bag. By the time he got downstairs to Inez, he knew what he had to do.

When Inez saw his face, she ground out her cigarette and hopped into the car. She didn't know what had happened, but she could tell it wasn't good.

"Where to?"

"Fountain, Inez. We've got to get one last shot."

Inez peeled out of the parking space and swerved into the street as Bondi slammed the door. "I'll get you there, kid," she muttered grimly. It was going to be close.

Melissa

"See? Eight stories." Tanisha stood on Michigan Avenue pointing up at the InterContinental Hotel building.

"Okay, you're right." Melissa aimed the camera at the frieze on the south wall. "It's those Sumerian warriors that are on the twelfth. I knew something was." The Inter-Continental Hotel had three Assyrian friezes on its facade: one called *Wisdom* on the west wall, *Consecration* on the north wall, and *Contribution*, guarded overhead by carvings of three Sumerian warriors, on the south wall. The friezes depicted the history of the building, from the funding of the building, aka the presentation of riches, in *Contribution*, to its construction in *Wisdom*, and the final dedication of the building, aka the anointing, in *Consecration*.

Melissa hesitated. "South, right? This one on the south wall is the right one?" The last thing she wanted to do was take a photo of the wrong stupid frieze.

Tanisha rolled her eyes. "Yes. South, the one with the horses that looks like a parade. You've only asked me like a million times."

"I know," Melissa muttered, taking the picture. She didn't even know why she was bothering. That Bondi kid had already won, according to Dimitri. And with Tanisha right here, she couldn't even pretend that she hadn't had help. But she'd figured out the three answers, so she was darn well going to finish. Maybe Mr. Smith would want to meet with her and maybe he wouldn't. But at least she'd tried.

She finished taking the last photo and then turned to Dimitri. "All done."

He smiled sadly. "I can call Mr. Smith?"

Melissa shrugged. "Sure. I can meet with him tomorrow, if there's still anything to meet about."

Tanisha smacked her on the arm. "Are you crazy? Meet him *today*! There's a one-hour photo place just down the block! Probably wouldn't even take that long."

Melissa shook her head. Liam was still at his friend's house, but he'd be getting back any minute. It wasn't safe for him to be home alone. And besides, she'd like to have one more night to imagine she could possibly win. Mr. Smith could tell her she'd lost tomorrow.

"Tomorrow's fine," she said. "He probably wouldn't want to meet this late, anyway."

Tanisha looked at her for a long minute and then shrugged. "Sure. Tomorrow."

Wilf

Wilf sprawled in the back of the car as Frank drove him home. He'd seen every animal in the zoo, some twice, even. He thought he had a good, friendly relationship started with one of the monkeys. And he'd had popcorn and cotton candy—although he'd paced himself a little more carefully this time.

Frank cleared his throat. "So that Bondi kid's solved all his clues, you know."

Wilf nodded. Frank had told him outside the lion house, and then again when they were looking at the boa constrictor. He didn't know why Frank was bringing it up again. It's not like Wilf wanted to talk about it. What was there to talk about? The Bondi kid won. Goody for him.

"Yeah, you said." Wilf pressed his forehead to the glass and looked out.

Frank drove in silence for a minute. "You want to talk about it?"

"No." Wilf breathed on the window and drew a frowny face in the condensation. "So . . . what? No more doing stuff, is that it? Or am I supposed to keep working on my clues, even though there's no point?"

Frank sighed. "I'm not sure. I'll find out."

Wilf wiped away his frowny face and stared out of the window. It had been good while it lasted, but with his track record, he'd always known it wouldn't last long. He had a knack for messing things up. It wasn't like he'd ever had a real shot at the money.

The only bad part was Frank. It was too bad that he wouldn't be able to hang out with him anymore. He was pretty cool, for a grown-up. And Wilf didn't think even his dad would've eaten as many hot dogs as Frank did. But now that it was all over, Frank would move on to some new assignment, and that would be that.

Wilf peered out of the window and then sat bolt upright. "Frank! Stop!"

Frank hit the brakes and pulled over, almost getting rear ended in the process.

"Geez, Wilf! What?"

He pointed out the window. They were across the street from an ancient-looking mansion made of pinkish brown stone, so big it took up half the block. "See that house there?"

"Yeah? So?"

"That's the Ambrose place, right? That old millionaire guy who died? Well, I heard it's haunted. They say his ghost haunts the house, and you can see lights and stuff moving around inside even though it's supposed to be totally empty. Freaky, huh?"

Frank sighed. "I hadn't heard that."

Wilf nodded. "It's true. So it's haunted, right? It's a haunted house." He leaned forward and peered at Frank around the headrest. "Want to sneak in? Maybe see the ghost? We could be ghost hunters! It would be really fun."

Frank shook his head. "No, Wilf. That's not a good idea."

Wilf bounced on the seat. Ghost hunting wasn't on his list, but it should've been. It was his best idea ever. "No, it's awesome. Because, Frank, this could be it! After tonight, there's no more anything. That kid won, so this is our last chance to do anything fun. Please, Frank?" Wilf held his breath. He'd never minded hanging out by himself before—he was used to it, with his dad always away and his mom having to work so much. But he'd never realized how much more fun it was to have someone to do things with.

Frank just shook his head again. "No, Wilf." He put the car back in drive. "Come on, I'll take you home."

"Fine. Whatever." Wilf threw himself against the backseat so hard he bounced a little. Frank was such a loser. Wilf didn't care if he never saw him again. Sure, the scholarship stuff had seemed fun once, but now he was glad the whole thing was over. It had all just been a stupid waste of time.

• •

Bondi

Bondi hopped out of the car and ran up to Buckingham Fountain, camera ready to go. The shots he'd gotten before were all silly, with him making goofy faces and messing around, but there'd be no messing around this time. He just needed one good shot of a spitty fish hugger or goose. Whichever one he saw first, that's what he'd take, and then he'd be out of there.

Bondi leaned in for a close-up of one of the fish spitting at the edge of the fountain, and then stopped. He looked through the camera lens, and after a few minutes of hesitation, he lowered the camera without taking the shot.

Those things spitting water in the corner weren't fish

at all. They were sea horses or something. Sea serpents, maybe, if you were pushing it. But definitely not fish, and now that he looked, they weren't hugging anything.

Bondi walked slowly around the edge of the fountain, examining it carefully from every angle. All he needed was one clear shot of a goose or fish. The cold feeling that had started creeping over his body had enveloped him completely by the time he got back to his original sea horse. Bondi clutched the short fence around the fountain, a sick, hollow feeling in the pit of his stomach.

Mr. Smith had said he'd gotten the answers right—all of them. That he'd solved the clues correctly. But now, watching the water splash against the stone, Bondi knew better.

Buckingham Fountain was the wrong fountain. It wasn't the solution to the clue. And Mr. Smith didn't know the answer was wrong.

Melissa

Liam was playing solitaire on Melissa's floor when she came in.

"So?" Liam said, a red 8 poised over a black 9.

"So what?" Melissa dumped her book bag on the floor and flopped down onto her bed.

Liam made a face at her. "So what happened? You're super late. Did you figure it out?"

Melissa mushed her face into her pillow. "Yes," she said, her voice muffled. "Yes, I figured it out."

"And?" Liam tugged on the hem of her jeans. "What happened? You have to tell—I had to spend the afternoon with stupid Arnie and his mom. They made cookies." Liam pretended to barf in Melissa's book bag. He hated Arnie's mom's cookies, but Gran said he had to eat at least one to be polite.

"Fine." Melissa unmushed her face and sat up. "Yes,

I figured it out. It's the InterContinental Hotel building. That's the solution to the third clue. The guy who played Tarzan used to swim inside at their super-fancy pool, and there's a big carving on the side of the building. But it doesn't matter. That other kid solved his clues first, so he won."

Liam dropped the cards onto the floor. "Did they say that? It's official?"

Melissa shrugged. "No. I don't know. It's weird. Dimitri still wants me to meet with the Smith guy tomorrow, but I don't know why. I guess I'll get the official bad news then."

"Yeah, I guess." Liam's chin quivered as he picked up the cards and quietly put them back in the box. Then he looked up at Melissa and punched her lightly on the sneaker. "That really stinks, huh."

Melissa tried to smile. She didn't even want to think about all the plans she'd had if she won. She'd tried so hard not to get her hopes up, but it had seemed like she had a real chance this time. Now everything would just go back to the way it was before.

Melissa punched Liam lightly back. "Yeah, it really stinks."

Bondi

Bondi did his best to seem relaxed as Mr. Smith looked over the photos for the second time. He had finally decided to take just a standard shot of Buckingham Fountain, but it was so obviously the wrong fountain that Bondi winced every time Smith looked at it. Smith had to know. Right? This had to be a test.

But Mr. Smith just stacked the photos in a neat pile and smiled at Bondi. "Excellent work, Master Johnson. Excellent. These new photos will be perfectly acceptable."

Bondi felt his tension evaporate. "So that means I win? I get the scholarship and everything?"

Mr. Smith kept smiling, but his eyes were hard. "Now, don't get ahead of yourself. First I must make sure that everything was done according to our rules and you haven't violated the contract in any way, shape, or form. Then and *only* then will I be in touch to discuss your standing in the competition. Until that point, I say a hearty thank-you. You've done good work, and good work is always a reward in itself, isn't it?"

Bondi frowned. "Well, yes, but—"

"As I said, if you haven't violated any clauses, terms, rules, et cetera, then you shouldn't have anything to worry about, should you? You haven't done anything to void our agreement, have you? You signed a legally binding document."

Bondi shook his head. He didn't think he had. Well, aside from that whole getting-the-answer-wrong thing.

Mr. Smith's smile got wider. "Then you will be hearing from us quite soon. Or at some point. In the future."

"Okay, great. So—"

Mr. Smith stood up. "Now Butler will show you out and relieve you of your competition materials. And thank you again for a job well done."

"Competition materials?"

"Cell phones, manuals, other accoutrement. All items relating to the competition must be returned at this time. Butler?" Mr. Smith snapped his fingers, and Mr. Butler appeared from the shadows of the room. He opened the door and stood next to it, looming over Bondi.

Bondi hesitated. He didn't want to stay, but he sure didn't want to leave—not without getting a better idea of what was going on. This sure didn't feel like winner treatment.

But he had a feeling that if he didn't go, Mr. Smith would be planting a foot on his butt and shoving him out.

"Yeah, okay." Bondi nodded coolly at Butler as he strolled into the boring outer office.

Mr. Butler followed, closing the door behind them. "If you'll give me just a moment, I'll escort you to the elevator, Mr. Johnson," he said, opening a small door and disappearing inside.

"No, that's oka—"

"You will wait, Mr. Johnson."

"Okay, I will wait," Bondi muttered. Like he wasn't able to show himself to the elevator. Bondi glanced around the generic office. It gave him the creeps. There wasn't anything personal about it at all. It felt wrong, like it was all fake. Just like the competition.

Mr. Butler came back out and put a hand on Bondi's back, gently ushering him out of the bland office and down the hallway to the elevators.

He pushed the elevator call button and smiled down at Bondi. "As Mr. Smith said, well done, Mr. Johnson." Mr. Butler's voice was oily and low.

"Thanks," Bondi said.

"So please accept this on behalf of my employer."

Mr. Butler held out a small cream-colored envelope with Bondi's name written in elaborate script on the front.

Bondi took it carefully. The envelope was made out

of heavy paper, and it looked important, formal. Not big enough for a check, though.

The elevator door opened, and Bondi looked up. "So I'm supposed to give you back the phone and stuff?"

Mr. Butler smiled. "In due time. Perhaps you will be needing them for just a short while longer."

Bondi shrugged and stepped into the elevator as the doors were closing. If Butler didn't care about him keeping the phone, he wasn't going to argue.

"So quick question," Bondi said, holding the elevator door open. "Mr. Smith—did he write those clues himself? I wouldn't blame him if he had help. Because they were pretty tough, let me tell you! Must be a pretty smart guy to have come up with those clues. How'd he come up with all that?"

Butler leaned into the elevator and smiled as he pushed the down button. "Good-bye, Mr. Johnson."

Bondi shrugged, and stepped back into the elevator. Once the doors had closed, he opened the heavy envelope. It was an invitation.

Your attendance is requested
3 P.M., at the Taj Mahal.

"Oh, sheesh." Bondi leaned against the elevator wall and groaned. *Taj Mahal.* Just when he thought things couldn't get any weirder.

191

Bondi shoved the card into his pocket and kicked a panel of the elevator. A plan had started forming in the back of his mind, and he didn't like it one bit. He didn't even know if it would work, but it wasn't like he had a lot of other ideas. By the time the elevator reached the lobby, he'd decided. He knew what he had to do.

• •

Melissa

Melissa's grandmother was just settling down with the remote when the phone rang.

"Oh, snackle crackbuckets," Gran said. "I just got comfy. Melissa, do you mind?"

Melissa swiveled on her heel and headed for the phone. "No problem." She picked up the receiver. "Hello?"

"Um, is Melissa Burris there?" The voice on the other end of the line was muffled; the reception was terrible.

"This is Melissa. Who is this?"

"Melissa Burris who's participating in a scholarship contest? With red hair?"

Melissa narrowed her eyes. She didn't like the sound of that one bit. "Who is this?" Melissa hissed, glancing at her grandmother as she ducked into the kitchen.

"Hey, Melissa, long time no speak. So anyway, this is Bondi Johnson. From the competition? Funny thing about that—"

"Yeah, I know who you are." Melissa took a deep breath. "So congratulations, I guess."

"What?"

Melissa gritted her teeth. She didn't know why Bondi was calling to rub things in, but she was going to be a good sport if it killed her. Be the bigger person. She faked a smile so her voice would sound extra happy. "Congratulations, on winning and all. That's really great. I mean, I was right behind you, figured out my clues tonight, but I guess the best man won."

"Oh. Well, thanks. But that's not why I—"

"So, look, I've got to go. Congrats again, and uh, good luck with everything. Bye." Melissa hung up abruptly and then leaned against the wall. At least that was over and she wouldn't have to be a good sport anymore. Well, after tomorrow, anyway. After she'd gone in and gotten the official bad news from Mr. Smith. Once she'd done that she could be a terrible sport and tiny, bitter person and spit nails if she wanted to. It sounded great to her.

"Friend of yours, Melissa?" Gran called from the other room.

"Sort of," Melissa said, tucking her hair behind her ears and putting on a happy face before heading back in. If someone you never want to see again counts as a friend.

"Well, come sit down now. The show's about to start! Tonight it's 'Enoch Ambrose: The Later Years.'"

"Can't wait," Melissa said. It was all Enoch Ambrose all the time in her house. She wasn't sure why he was rating multiple nights on prime time, but whatever. At least she wouldn't have to talk or be chipper for the hour it was on.

Bondi

Bondi glared at the phone. It hadn't been easy tracking down Melissa's phone number, and convincing Inez to leave him alone while he made the call to his "dad" had been even trickier. He hadn't expected Melissa to be thrilled to hear from him, but he figured she'd at least let him get two words in edgewise. Talk about a sore loser.

Bondi slipped the phone back into his pocket and headed out of the building. Inez was leaning against the car, flicking her lighter on and off and looking bored.

"Kid, you didn't even say— Did he give you your prize?" Inez asked, flipping her lighter into the air and then pocketing it in one smooth motion.

"Not exactly." Bondi dumped his messenger bag in the back of the car.

"Well, Butler called and said that I'm still your driver for the next week or so, so that's a bonus, right? You're probably raring to hit the town?"

"No, I just want to go home. But yeah, it's a bonus," Bondi said, slipping his hand into his jacket pocket. The invitation was still there. He didn't mention it to Inez, though. It wasn't like she could give him a ride to the Taj Mahal, after all. Or tell him when he was supposed to go there.

And as cool as Inez was, he wasn't about to tell her any more secrets. Not until he knew where she fit into this whole thing. And how much she wasn't telling *him*.

Melissa

Melissa put her feet up on the coffee table just as "Enoch Ambrose: The Later Years" came back on.

"So how old is he supposed to be now?" Melissa scanned the coffee table for snackies, but there weren't any.

Gran frowned. "Well, you missed 'Enoch Ambrose: A Golden Time,' and 'Enoch Ambrose: Businessman Extraordinaire.' That one featured his feud with Colonel McCormick of the *Tribune*. So I think he's probably in his sixties in this one? Or maybe older? Who cares? He looks good at any age!"

Melissa nodded and tried not to cringe when Gran squealed as Enoch Ambrose appeared on the screen.

What Melissa needed was popcorn. Popcorn would get her through this. She had to have something to munch on if she was going to pretend to enjoy this boring history stuff.

"Popcorn, Gran?" Melissa said, pushing the afghan off her knees.

"Ooh, yes, please. Look! There he is at the lake house! So dashing." Gran sighed.

Melissa made approving noises and headed into the kitchen. She wished that Bondi kid hadn't called. She'd been feeling pretty okay with things up until then. Sure, she was nervous about her meeting, but it wasn't that bad. Now she just felt twisted and weird inside.

The popcorn didn't look too bad when she had finished microwaving it—only half of the kernels were burned, and she hadn't set off the smoke detector or anything. She dumped the bag into a big plastic bowl and carried it into the living room.

"Here you go! Nice, fresh, hot pop—" Melissa stopped abruptly and stared at the TV.

Enoch Ambrose was sitting at a picnic table and smoking a cigar. A pinch-faced woman was next to him, and a sour-looking man was fanning himself with a hat.

Melissa pointed at the screen. "Who . . . who is that?"

"Why, that's Enoch, hon." Gran stared at her in concern. "Who else? And those are his children, Linus and Sybil. Don't worry, you haven't missed too much. You can catch up."

Melissa didn't even notice as her grandmother took the popcorn bowl out of her hand. She just gaped at the screen.

"Sit, honey?" Gran patted the couch next to her.

Melissa shook her head and wandered back into the kitchen. "I have to make a call," she said as she disappeared into the other room.

She leaned against the countertop, pressing her forehead against the wall. That photo showed Enoch Ambrose and his children, Linus and Sybil. Melissa had never officially met any of the Ambrose family. But she'd seen Linus Ambrose more than once. She'd even spoken to him.

Only she'd called him Mr. Smith.

Thursday

Melissa's Clues:

> Go to the site of Lorado Taft's Death in 1909.

> Freeze! Look to the building where Tarzan swam to find your "Contribution."

> Go to 1910 for ice cream, then stick around to watch the newborns.

Wilf's Clues:

> Jeremiah 6:23 plus Psalm 46:9

> Madame Tussaud and Mrs. O'Leary would be proud of their little blue friend.

> ???

Bondi's Invitation:

Your attendance is requested
3 P.M., at the Taj Mahal.

Wilf

Wilf slammed the apartment door with a *boom* and headed downstairs, swinging himself along using the railings. He had to hustle to catch the bus, even though that was the last thing he wanted to ride. It was surprising how quickly you could get used to having someone drive you everywhere. Especially when the bus on your route smelled like a combination of gas, rotten tuna fish, and sweat.

Wilf kicked the building's front door open and jumped down the entrance steps, almost slamming into some guy standing in the middle of the sidewalk.

"Sorry," he muttered. But really, what kind of guy just stands in the middle of the sidewalk?

"What, forget me already?"

Wilf looked up and broke into a surprised grin. "Frank?"

Frank shrugged. "Funny thing, looks like they want you to keep going with those clues, anyway."

"Even though that Bondi kid won?"

"Even though." Frank reached into his pocket and pulled out a folded-up piece of paper. "So we're going to have to get moving if we want to finish up before I'm reassigned. So what's next?" He scanned the page. "Seadog boat trip?"

Wilf grinned. "You said it, Skipper."

• •

Melissa

Melissa waved good-bye to Dimitri and hurried into the school, trying to act normal. But once she was through the door, she pressed herself against the wall and peeked out of the window, watching until Dimitri drove away.

"You okay, Burris?" Troy Cantrell was staring at her like she'd grown two heads.

"You didn't see a thing, got it, Cantrell?" Melissa glared at him.

Troy went white. "Got it. Didn't see a thing."

Melissa slipped back out of the front doors, nervously checking behind her every few seconds as she made her way down the street. She didn't relax until she was safely inside the coffee shop down the block.

Bondi was sitting at one of the tables, just like he said he'd be when she'd called him back the night before. He was eating a chocolate doughnut and drinking what looked like some kind of tea. At least he'd been smart enough to get a table in the corner, away from the window.

Melissa dumped her book bag on one of the empty chairs and flopped down. "You realize if we're spotted we'll both be disqualified. It's in the rules. Rule number two, I believe."

Bondi nodded. "I don't think it even matters. Something is seriously wrong with this whole competition."

Melissa snorted. "Tell me about it. You saw the documentary, too?"

Bondi frowned. "Documentary? I was talking about the clues and Mr. Smith."

Melissa snorted again. "Mr. Smith? Right. Mr. *Ambrose*, you mean."

"Whoa, Nelly, slow down. What documentary? Who's Mr. Ambrose?" After Melissa had agreed to meet with him, Bondi had planned how he would break the news about Mr. Smith and the clues. He'd worked out exactly what he would say and how it would go. This wasn't how it was supposed to go.

Melissa nodded. "You didn't see it? It was on last night. 'Enoch Ambrose: The Later Years.' They showed a picture of him with his kids. And guess what? Mr. Smith is really Linus Ambrose, that millionaire guy's son."

Bondi whistled. Of all the things he'd expected her to say, it wasn't that. "Man, that's messed up." He frowned and inspected his doughnut. "That's really messed up. But you know, it makes total sense. I *knew* that guy was one hundred percent shady!"

Melissa eyed Bondi's doughnut, too. "Shady and creepy. But wait, if you didn't know he was Linus Ambrose, what are you talking about? What's wrong with the competition?"

Bondi put his elbows on the table and leaned forward. "It's big."

"So tell me."

"Really big. You might need a doughnut."

"Forget the doughnut, okay? Just say it." It killed her to say that, but she wanted him to spit it out.

Bondi took a deep breath. "Okay. I solved all my clues, right?"

Melissa nodded. "Yeah, way to rub it in."

Bondi shook his head. "No—that's the thing. I got one of them *wrong*."

Melissa was surprised her jaw didn't hit the table. "What

do you mean you got it wrong? You didn't win? What am I doing here? Is this a setup?" It was one thing to break the rules when Bondi was the winner, but if she still had a shot? That was completely different.

"No, listen: *I got an answer wrong*," Bondi said, tapping the table with each word. "And Mr. Smith—Mr. Ambrose, I guess—*he didn't know*."

"He didn't know it was wrong?" Melissa said under her breath. "What do you mean? How could he not know it was wrong? It's his competition!"

Bondi shook his head. "He thought it was right."

Melissa rubbed her forehead. "I need a doughnut."

Bondi grinned. "I thought you might. Just a sec." He hopped up and headed for the counter while Melissa lay her head down on the table. She didn't pick it up again until Bondi was back, waving a chocolate-glazed under her nose.

She sat up. Nothing revives like a doughnut. "So what you're saying is that we're solving these clues . . ."

"Yep."

". . . that Mr. Smith gave us . . ."

"Yep."

". . . and he doesn't know what the answers are."

"Right."

"And you're sure?"

"Totally sure."

"So what are we doing?" Melissa took an angry bite of

doughnut. "This isn't a scholarship competition, is it?"

Bondi shook his head. "I don't think so. I think this is something else."

Melissa slammed her fist down onto the table. "*What the heck?* So what is this, some kind of scam? What are the clues for, then? What are we solving? Ouch." She massaged her hand.

"That's what we're going to find out. You still have your meeting today, right? To turn in your answers?"

Melissa nodded.

"Okay, so turn yours in just like you would've. And that'll tell us two things. First, we'll see if Butler gives you one of these."

He handed her the invitation.

Melissa inspected the card. "Taj Mahal? What does it mean?"

Bondi took the card back and looked at it closely. "Beats me. He gave it to me in the hallway, afterward. I want to see if you get the same one. And then we'll figure out what they're up to."

"How are we going to do that?"

Bondi smiled. "Simple. I'll follow them."

Wilf

NOTE TO SELF:
BUY MOTION-SICKNESS PILLS FOR
FUTURE ACTIVITIES (JUST IN CASE).

TENTATIVE SCHEDULE, WILF SAMSON: (UPDATED)

1. ~~Go to aquarium.~~

2. ~~Visit Sears Tower Skydeck Ledge (Willis Tower, whatever).~~

3. Watch laser light show at the planetarium.

4. ~~Go to zoo (both Lincoln Park and Brookfield, if possible).~~

5. ~~Ride Ferris wheel at Navy Pier.~~

6. Seadog boat ride.

7. ~~Hot Dog taste-test-a-thon—Fat Johnnie's vs. Wiener's~~
   ~~Circle vs. Jimmy's Red Hots vs. Superdawg vs. others~~
   ~~to be named later (until puking commences)~~ PUKING
   COMPLETE.

8. Get psychic reading.

ALSO: FIGURE OUT CLUES AND SOLUTIONS.

9. ~~GO SKYDIVING.~~ Vetoed by Frank.

~~10. Take helicopter tour.~~ Unexpected fear of heights. Who knew?

11. Kayak on Chicago River.

12. Play bubble soccer (first, figure out what exactly bubble soccer is).

Notes on Car Service Garage Chalkboard:

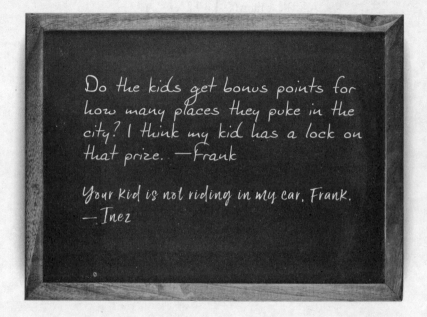

Do the kids get bonus points for how many places they puke in the city? I think my kid has a lock on that prize. —Frank

Your kid is not riding in my car, Frank. —Inez

Bondi: Did research at lunch—I found the right fountain.

Bondi: It's called the Eli Bates Fountain, or Storks at Play, and there's a ton of fish hugging and spitty storks that look like geese. You've got to see it.

Melissa: Great.

Bondi: And I think I figured out the invitation. There's a restaurant in University Village called Taj Mahal. After you get your invite and I finish my stakeout, we can head over.

Bondi: Hope I'm done by 3 p.m., so we don't miss the appointment.

Melissa: ZIP IT! These phones may not be secure!

Bondi: Wait, this is Melissa Burke, right? I think I have the wrong Melissa. I'm working on a thing. For English. Just brainstorming made-up ideas that are fake. And made-up. You know, for school.

Melissa: Real slick. They'll never suspect a thing.

Melissa

Melissa shifted nervously as Mr. Smith looked at the photos she'd taken. She'd thought they were pretty awesome, but spread out on his desk, they all looked kind of lousy. Her composition was all off, and the lighting was all over the place.

Melissa swallowed hard. *Composition?* She didn't even know what she was talking about.

"Clue one! Solution!" Mr. Smith barked.

Melissa jumped and then glared at Mr. Smith. She bet he hadn't been this much of a jerk with Bondi. "*Eternal Silence* statue, also known as the statue of Death, in Graceland Cemetery. It was a trick question, see, because—"

"Clue two! Solution!" Mr. Smith barked again, his eyes gleaming. He was enjoying himself way too much. He looked down at the paper. "*Freeze! Look to the building where Tarzan swam to find your 'Contribution.'* Answer!"

"That's the InterContinental Hotel, the frieze on the south wall." Melissa focused on the space in between Mr. Smith's eyes. If she looked him full in the face, she thought she might slug him.

"Clue—"

"AND CLUE NUMBER THREE," Melissa said in a loud voice, cutting him off, "is the Museum of Science and Industry, the baby chicks hatchery and the ice cream parlor."

Mr. Smith narrowed his eyes. "Baby chicks?"

"Baby chicks."

"How can that be the solution? Baby chicks are ridiculous," Mr. Smith huffed, as though he thought Melissa had invented baby chicks.

"Go to 1910 for ice cream—that's Finnigan's, which is on that old-timey Main Street in the museum. And the baby chicks are the only newborns there. If you can find newborns having ice cream somewhere else, go with that answer, be my guest."

Mr. Smith glared at her for a long minute, then looked at the photo she'd taken of the baby chick. It was the particularly slimy newborn. Melissa had made a duplicate of the photo for herself.

Mr. Smith drew himself up tall in his seat and folded his arms.

"Very good, young lady," he said, staring down the bridge

of his nose at her. "Well done. Butler? Collect her items and see her out."

Melissa refused to budge. "So I'm what, second place?"

Mr. Smith sighed loudly. "As I told the young man yesterday, every attempt will be made to ensure that you followed the rules *at all times* and that you have maintained an unquestionable character. Only then will the scholarship money be awarded. And believe me, your actions will be subjected to the highest scrutiny." He waved his hand at her like he thought he could flick her away.

Melissa still didn't move.

"We will be in touch at some point in the future with your standings. Butler?"

Mr. Butler held the door open again, took Melissa by the shoulder, and propelled her out into the hall.

She stalked to the elevators without a word and held out the ziplock bag with the cell phone and debit card.

Mr. Butler smiled and held up a hand. "That won't be necessary quite yet." He reached into his pocket and took out an envelope. "Please accept this on behalf of my employer."

Melissa took the envelope. Her name was written on it in elaborate script. "Okay. Thanks."

"Until we meet again, Miss Burris."

The elevator door opened. Melissa took a step toward it and then hesitated. "So these offices, are they your usual digs? I mean, they seem kind of impersonal, if you know what I mean. Is Mr. Smith some kind of businessman or something? I've never heard of him. But you know, Smith. Pretty common name. What's his first name? John?"

Mr. Butler reached out and stopped the elevator door just as it was about to close. "Until we meet again, Miss Burris." His smile never faltered.

Melissa nodded and then, after a minute, stepped into the elevator.

Guess that was too much to hope for, she said to herself, tearing open the envelope.

Your attendance is requested
This Monday, Clementine Hall,
Pope's Residence.

Melissa groaned as she dialed her cell phone. "Bondi, I got my invitation, and you're not going to like this. It's different. It's not the Taj Mahal."

Wilf

> **Frank:** Wilf, what do you say we skip the more active plans on the list? I'm not sure my stomach can take much more.

> **Wilf:** Don't sugarcoat it, Frank. If you think I'm a puker, just say I'm a puker.

> **Frank:** You're a puker, kid. A good puker, but a puker.

Bondi

B ondi fiddled with the handlebars of one of the bikes in the Divvy bike-share rack. Melissa had left the office building an hour ago, but so far there hadn't been any sign of Mr. Butler or Mr. Smith. If he hadn't been watching so carefully, Bondi would've thought he missed them, but there was no way they could've snuck past the stakeout king.

After he'd heard about Melissa's invitation, he'd scrapped his Taj Mahal restaurant idea. He couldn't make it out there and also keep an eye on the office. Besides, he had a feeling Butler and Smith would lead him wherever he needed to go. If that turned out to be the Taj Mahal restaurant, so be it. But that didn't mean he wanted to sit around all night.

Bondi had just hopped up to test out one of the bike seats when a black car pulled up in front of the building. He didn't recognize the driver, but he sure recognized the car. He and the other two kids had been riding around in those all week.

Bondi slid off the bike seat and unlocked the bike. He'd just pulled it into the street when a man emerged from the building and walked toward the waiting car. There was no mistaking Butler. Smith was probably right behind him.

"Hey, are you using that one?"

Bondi jerked his head around. Some guy in a Phish T-shirt had his hand on the handlebars of Bondi's bike. Bondi glared at him. "Jeez, buddy, back off. Use a different bike, okay? This one's mine."

"Sorry, okay, sheesh." The guy held up his hands and slowly stepped away like he was afraid Bondi was going to bite him.

Bondi glared at the guy until he had picked a different bike from the rack and then turned back to the waiting car. He was just in time to see the door slam shut.

Bondi bent down and pretended to fiddle with his bike chain until the car pulled past him. He didn't want to lose them, but he didn't want to follow too closely, especially with the headlight on the bike flashing like a beacon. One thing about those Divvy bikes, they weren't inconspicuous. But they were common, and Bondi hoped that one more wouldn't attract attention, even if it was right on their tail.

Besides, a flashing light was the least of his problems. If

they turned onto the highway, he'd never be able to keep up. He'd be done before he'd even gotten started.

Bondi coasted up the block, swerving to avoid a panicky squirrel and a car door that opened in front of him, all the while keeping the black car a half a block ahead. He hoped this wasn't the world's stupidest idea. But he had to know where they were going.

He was so intent on keeping his distance that he almost didn't notice when the car slowed down and pulled up in front of the huge stone mansion up ahead. Bondi stopped and watched, then did a silent fist pump. Bingo. It was the Ambrose mansion, just like they'd suspected. There was no way Mr. Smith could deny his identity now, not with photographic evidence. Which was exactly what Bondi planned to get.

He pulled his phone out of his pocket and waited as Butler stepped out of the car and headed up the thick stone steps. Bondi didn't have the best angle, though, and a gust of wind blew some branches into the frame, so he didn't get a shot of Smith going in with him.

The car pulled away down the street and disappeared around the corner. Bondi hesitated for a moment and then pedaled closer to the house. The car was not important, not if Butler and Smith weren't inside it. He needed a photo of *them*, not the car going back to some dumb garage.

Bondi grinned. It was one thing to see it himself, but

it was something else to get irrefutable proof. He ditched the bike at the nearest Divvy stand and snuck down the street.

The house was huge, made of ancient, expensive-looking stone, complete with towers and gates, the whole shebang. He'd seen it a million times on TV, but never up close. This wasn't exactly his neighborhood.

Bondi crept up the stone steps onto the porch, trying to look both casual and inconspicuous, which isn't easy when you're sliding along a wall. Then he quickly peeked into the window on the first floor. He had a bad feeling the peeking part hadn't been all that inconspicuous, since he'd had to kind of lean out over a stone ledge to get a look. But nobody was shouting at him or running him off the property, so that had to be a good sign.

Bondi had to admit, he was surprised they'd actually gone inside. Word was that the place was haunted and totally deserted. He'd thought it was supposed to be off-limits until the will stuff was all sorted out—that's what Melissa had told him, anyway. She'd seen it on the news.

Bondi leaned farther. He couldn't see anyone moving inside, but that didn't mean they weren't there. He held out his phone to try to get a shot of the interior, and just as he did, the curtain snapped open. Bondi jumped, taking the picture as he jerked his hand back and took off running down the block. He didn't stop until he was a good three or four blocks away and had spent a little quality time hiding out in the shampoo section of Walgreens.

Once he was sure he hadn't been followed, he slowly took out his phone and looked to see what he'd taken a picture of. It was blurry, and it was off-center, but it didn't matter. Bondi knew what it was.

It was Butler. He'd been spotted.

To: Inez Castillo, Frank Jennings, Dimitri Omar
From: Butler
Subject: Reports due ASAP

Progress reports, please. What are your children interested in, investigating, etc.?
Just consider this a little healthy interest on the part of my employer.

Butler

To: Butler, Frank Jennings, Dimitri Omar
From: Inez Castillo
Subject: RE: Reports due ASAP

My kid just won. Don't they keep you in the loop?

To: Inez Castillo, Butler, Dimitri Omar
From: Frank Jennings
Subject: RE: Reports due ASAP

Slow but steady wins the race. My kid is taking it slow.

To: Frank Jennings, Butler, Dimitri Omar

From: Inez Castillo

Subject: RE: Reports due ASAP

Yeah, sure, except my kid just won. What's with you people?

To: Butler, Frank Jennings, Inez Castillo

From: Dimitri Omar

Subject: RE: Reports due ASAP

My kid also just won. So I will not be seeing her anymore, unless there are new requirements? I will be happy to continue if possible.

To: Dimitri Omar, Frank Jennings, Butler

From: Inez Castillo

Subject: RE: Reports due ASAP

WHAT PART OF "MY KID JUST WON" DON'T YOU UNDERSTAND? Your kid didn't win, Dimitri. You guys take the cake.

To: Inez Castillo, Dimitri Omar, Frank Jennings
From: Butler
Subject: RE: Reports due ASAP

Thank you for your updates. You will continue with
your assigned child until further notice. And until the
winner is determined, Inez.

To: Butler, Dimitri Omar, Frank Jennings
From: Inez Castillo
Subject: RE: Reports due ASAP

Sure, until my kid is declared the winner.

Melissa

Melissa peered at the blurry picture of Butler on Mrs. Lewis's computer screen. Or at least Bondi claimed it was Butler. She was going to have to take his word for that.

"So he saw you?" she whispered into the cell phone. "You're sure? I mean *sure* sure?" She was across the hall at Mrs. Lewis's house, printing out the latest scam e-mails, including one from Svetlana in Ukraine, and weirdly enough, one from Saddam Hussein's daughter. Turns out she wanted to give Mrs. Lewis five million dollars, and all Mrs. Lewis had to do was wire her two thousand dollars to pay for the bank transfer. Melissa deleted that one. There were some things Mrs. Lewis just didn't need to see.

"Did you see the picture? Of *course* he saw me!" Bondi didn't bother keeping his voice down. His parents were both at their macramé art class and wouldn't be back for another hour.

Melissa looked closer at the picture. "He saw your hand, sure. And the phone. But did he know it was yours?"

Bondi groaned. "Come *on*. How dumb do you think he is? I'm the only black kid in this competition, Melissa. He and Smith both know it was me."

Melissa zoomed in on the picture. "Yeah, about that . . . I don't see Smith in this picture anywhere." As far as she could tell, Bondi's picture only showed some curtains and one "person," which was being generous, definition-wise.

"That doesn't mean he's not there, Melissa." Bondi's voice was shrill through the phone. "Did you see the picture? This proves everything!"

Melissa printed an e-mail promising Mrs. Lewis secret weight-loss tips and snorted into the phone. "This doesn't prove anything! Get real, Bondi. We don't have a photo of Smith in the house. We don't know what those invitations are for, or where we're supposed to go, or when. We don't know why they're using secret names, and we don't know why we're answering clues. *We know nothing*." She sighed. "Except that Butler is connected to the Ambrose family, and Smith is Linus Ambrose. We do know that. That's something."

"Well, when you put it that way . . ." Bondi grumbled. "So what do we do now?"

"We figure out what those invites are for," Melissa said, grumpily deleting the last ten spam messages to Mrs. Lewis unread. "Too bad we don't have the one for that other kid. It would be nice to know whether it said Taj Mahal or the Pope's Residence, or if he has something completely different."

"High five! That's a great idea!" Bondi was so loud Melissa had to take the phone away from her ear.

"What? What's a great idea?" Melissa was almost afraid to ask. She could practically hear Bondi strutting around on the other end.

"You just said it," Bondi said. "We get the other kid. This isn't a two-man job. It's a three-man job."

Melissa sucked in her breath. "Wait, do you mean . . . ?"

"Oh yeah. Tomorrow, we go get Wilf."

Friday

Wilf's Clues:

Jeremiah 6:23 plus Psalm 46:9

*Madame Tussaud and Mrs. O'Leary would
be proud of their little blue friend.*

???

Bondi's Invitation:

*Your attendance is requested
3 P.M., at the Taj Mahal.*

Melissa's Invitation:

*Your attendance is requested
This Monday, Clementine Hall,
Pope's Residence.*

Wilf, Bondi, and Melissa

"So this is all some kind of con?" Wilf perched uncomfortably on Bondi's couch. It was super low and squishy and smelled like potpourri, and his elbows and knees seemed to be competing with each other for space.

"Right!" Bondi looked relieved. Wilf hadn't said a thing the whole time he and Melissa had been explaining, and it was beginning to feel a little weird.

"Total con," Melissa said, peeking outside through the crack in the curtains. She didn't really expect Butler or Smith to show up at Bondi's front door, but you could never be too careful. "They're using us for something."

Bondi nodded slowly and smiled at Wilf. "Yeah, so we're teaming up, right? I mean, this is completely against the rules. But we don't care about that, right, Red?"

"Right." Melissa gave the street one last once-over and then sat in a high-backed chair with her arms folded. "We just have to figure out what their game is."

"Right . . ." Wilf echoed, looking from Bondi to Melissa and then back again. And then he broke out in a huge grin.

"Come on, for real?" Wilf said. *"Come on!"*

"For real," Bondi said.

Wilf shook his bangs out of his eyes. "No way! You guys are whacked-out!" He pointed at Bondi and Melissa, still grinning. "It's you guys, right? You're pulling a fast one on me?"

Melissa rolled her eyes. "No. For real, Wilf. The letter, the competition, the clues . . . they're just trying to get information from us."

Wilf shook his head again. "No way! That letter was real. It was sponsored by Kaplan! And Barron! Everybody's heard of those guys. They do those college guides and SAT things! They're totally legit."

Bondi pulled out his notification letter. "No, check it out. See here?" He pointed at the words. "It says *Kaplin* and *Baron*. They're spelled wrong."

Wilf shrugged. "Yeah, but those are probably just typos."

Bondi shot Melissa a look. "Okay, let's say they're typos. Go to the website for the scholarship. I looked up the site's history, and it was put up the day before we got the letters. And the links on it don't go anywhere—they're fakes."

"Plus, you can't find it on Google. It doesn't show up anywhere else except for that site," Melissa said.

Bondi pushed Wilf over to the computer on his dad's desk and then folded his arms. Wilf looked at the site, then at the letter, then back at the site. "Huh."

"You didn't ever get the feeling that something was weird?" Bondi asked. "They gave us drivers, phones, and debit cards. That's not normal."

Wilf grinned. "No, but it was cool!" Then his face darkened. "But . . ."

"What?" Bondi pounced as Wilf hesitated.

"I knew it! Something *was* weird, right?" Melissa said, jumping up.

"It's nothing. Just this one time. I kind of felt like . . ." He looked at the ground awkwardly. "It kind of felt like Frank was helping me with the clue. You know, like he knew the answer already."

Bondi whistled. "Seriously?"

Wilf nodded.

"Man, that *is* weird," said Melissa.

"But they don't know, do they? Why would Frank know?"

"He's not supposed to know, I'm pretty sure," Bondi said. "Inez tried to help me once, but she didn't know squat." He clenched his jaw. "Or at least she acted like she didn't."

"Sounds typical to me," Melissa said. "That's why we need you now. We need your clues."

"My, uh, clues?" Wilf swallowed hard.

"Right. How close are you to being done? We want to try something at your meeting with Mr. Smith, if you're okay with it."

Wilf shifted miserably. "Yeah, well, about my clues. I've been . . . exploring a couple of . . . See, I have this idea that . . ."

"How many, Wilf? How many clues solved?" Melissa said, snapping her fingers at him.

"One."

"One left?"

"One solved."

Melissa gawked at him. "*One solved?* How could you only have one solved?"

"I've been busy, okay?" Wilf shrugged. "I've got things to do."

Bondi put a hand on Melissa's shoulder. She looked like she was about to launch herself at Wilf, and that wouldn't lead to anything good. Bondi smiled encouragingly at Wilf. "Okay, one solved. That's fine. And we know it's right, because Frank . . . helped."

Wilf nodded.

"So we'll just figure out the other two and go from there. Do you have them with you?"

Wilf nodded and pulled out his envelope. "They're right here."

He opened the envelope and emptied the contents onto the coffee table. Two slips of paper fell out.

"Two. That's two, Wilf."

Wilf peered into the envelope. "Um, I guess I left the other one at home. I'll get it, though."

Bondi nodded and looked at the clues. *"Jeremiah 6:23 plus Psalm 46:9."*

"That's the one I solved."

Melissa snorted. "Of course it is."

"It's the *Bowman* and *Spearman* statues on Congress, downtown."

"Good," Bondi said, shooting Melissa a look. "Now, how about this one? *Madame Tussaud and Mrs. O'Leary would be proud of their little blue friend.* You have any ideas about that one?"

Wilf shrugged. "Maybe look up Mrs. O'Leary and see if she knows a Madame Tussaud?"

"Oh good grief," Melissa said. "Do you even *live* in Chicago? Mrs. O'Leary's cow, numskull! It's got to be something about a cow."

"Yeah, but cows aren't blue, genius," Wilf scoffed. She had a point, though. When he was at Navy Pier, he'd seen a store that was 90 percent cow stuff.

"Okay, good, Mrs. O'Leary's cow. We've got a starting point, so it's practically solved." Bondi shot Melissa another look and she shrugged and leaned back in her chair. "Do you remember the third clue?"

Had he even looked at the third clue? Wilf shook his head. "Sorry."

"Fine, no problem. So we figure out the clues, and then, once you've got a meeting set up, we spring into action. Sound good?"

Wilf nodded. Bondi raised his eyebrows at Melissa and after a few seconds she nodded, too. "Sure." Sounded more like impossible, if they were relying on Wilf. But she decided not to say anything.

"When you find that third clue, give me a call and tell me what it is. Or better yet, send me a picture of it," Bondi said, walking Wilf over to the kitchen island, where Wilf had dumped his backpack.

"Photo. Got it." Wilf grabbed his backpack and then picked up a Tupperware container on the counter. "What's this?"

Bondi set his jaw. "It's kale salad."

Wilf opened the container and sniffed the contents. "Weird."

"Yeah, I know, right?" Bondi snatched the Tupperware away from Wilf. "It's this Paleo diet thing my mom's doing. Don't even go there."

Wilf leaned over to peer into the container. "No, I mean, you didn't include any corn? And it smells like you left out the maple syrup, too. That's not the way I usually make it."

Bondi put down the container slowly. "The way you make it? What, you cook?"

Wilf shrugged. "I took a few classes. You know, since my mom . . . she's got stuff to do." He glared at Bondi. "What, you have something to say about it?"

"Sure do." Bondi grinned and opened the refrigerator. "Can you teach me? This stuff is killing me."

To: Bondi Johnson

From: Melissa Burris

Subject: Did we make a mistake?

I've got a bad feeling about this kid.

To: Melissa Burris

From: Bondi Johnson

Subject: RE: Did we make a mistake?

Give him a chance. The clue's probably just on his dresser or something. Besides, his kale salad is the bomb.

To: Bondi Johnson

From: Melissa Burris

Subject: RE: Did we make a mistake?

And what about the drivers? Dimitri is going to notice that I'm not calling him. He's very protective. Do you know how hard it is to sneak past that guy?

To: Melissa Burris

From: Bondi Johnson

Subject: RE: Did we make a mistake?

Relax. Dimitri probably hasn't even noticed yet.

To: Inez Castillo
From: Dimitri Omar
Subject: My kid is not calling.

Has your Bondi contacted you? I have heard nothing from Melissa since her meeting.

To: Dimitri Omar
From: Inez Castillo
Subject: RE: My kid is not calling.

Nope. Nothing. But no biggie, right? He won.

To: Dimitri Omar
From: Inez Castillo
Subject: RE: My kid is not calling.

It is weird, though.

To: Dimitri Omar
From: Inez Castillo
Subject: RE: My kid is not calling.

Something's up, isn't it?

To: Frank Jennings, Dimitri Omar

From: Inez Castillo

Subject: RE: My kid is not calling.

Okay, Frank, have you heard from your kid? Me and Dimitri are getting the cold shoulder. And it's freaking us out.

To: Frank Jennings, Inez Castillo

From: Dimitri Omar

Subject: RE: My kid is not calling.

Yes. I am freaking.

To: Inez Castillo, Dimitri Omar

From: Frank Jennings

Subject: RE: My kid is not calling.

Not a peep. But we'll get to the bottom of this. Tomorrow we'll meet with Butler.

HEY MOM,
    DID YOU FIND A LITTLE PIECE OF PAPER IN MY ROOM ANYWHERE? IT HAD SOME OLD-TIMEY LOOKING WRITING ON IT. I NEED IT FOR A SCHOOL THING.

                        THANKS,
                        WILF

Sorry, hon, I haven't seen anything like that.

Saturday

Wilf's Clues:

Jeremiah 6:23 plus Psalm 46:9

Madame Tussaud and Mrs. O'Leary would be proud of their little blue friend.

???

Bondi's Invitation:

Your attendance is requested 3 P.M., at the Taj Mahal.

Melissa's Invitation:

Your attendance is requested This Monday, Clementine Hall, Pope's Residence.

Wilf, Bondi, and Melissa

"So I think I figured out something with the Mrs. O'Leary clue," Melissa said, taking a bite of doughnut.

She couldn't believe this place had been down the block from her school all this time and she'd never hung out there before. But then, she'd never had extra money to spend on doughnuts or hang out in coffee shops or things like that. She'd been worried about buying too much, but Bondi seemed pretty sure they weren't going to have to reimburse Butler or Smith for their debit card purchases. It was pretty awesome to be able to get anything she wanted. Especially since Bondi liked to act like a big spender and put everything on his card.

"What did you figure out? Something about the cow?" Bondi wiped a piece of stray doughnut off of his jacket sleeve. Melissa wasn't the neatest eater.

"No, Madame Tussaud. I had a feeling I'd heard the

name before. That's the wax museum lady, isn't she?"

"Oh man, you're right," Wilf said, taking a doughnut from the box. It was his third. He figured if he had to get up this early on a Saturday *and* take the bus, he was entitled to half the doughnuts. At least.

Bondi nodded. "What was the clue again?"

Wilf dug the paper out of his pocket. *"Madame Tussaud and Mrs. O'Leary would be proud of their little blue friend."*

"So if they have the same friend, and we're assuming that Mrs. O'Leary's friend is a cow, that means—"

"We're looking for a cow. Probably made of wax. And blue." Wilf snickered, dropping the last part of his doughnut into his mouth. He wasn't the neatest eater, either. "But which blue wax cow? There are so many!" He snickered again.

Bondi set his jaw. "We need a computer."

"Why does it have to be a wax cow?" Melissa said gloomily. "A regular cow, we could do."

"Even I've seen regular cows. I just saw one the other day, in fact," Wilf said.

Melissa thunked her head against the back of her chair. "And why does it have to be a *cow*? Wax submarine I could do. Wax tractor, done. But who's seen a wax cow?"

Bondi frowned and closed the doughnut box before Wilf could take another one. He didn't know how many Wilf had eaten, but he didn't want to find out whether his stomach was really as weak as Inez said it was. "What do you mean, you saw a wax submarine? Where was that?"

"Museum of Science and Industry," Melissa said. "They had one of those thingies—you know, those machines that make wax figurines while you wait. Tanisha's sister, Tabi, wanted one, but we didn't have enough change."

"Oh yeah, those! I've seen those. Except I think they're made of plastic instead of wax," Wilf said, eyeing the doughnut box.

"Smelled like wax to me," Melissa said, raising an eyebrow. She didn't really care if it was melty plastic or wax or molten lava, if Wilf wanted to get into it, he was going down.

"You know, I *just* saw one of those. They had one . . . where?" Wilf pressed his fingers to his forehead, like it would help him think. "They had one at . . . somewhere. At the . . ."

Bondi caught his breath just as Wilf looked up, his eyes wide.

"THE ZOO!" they both said at the same time, high-fiving each other.

"The farm at the zoo. It's in the barn, right?" Bondi said. "I'm almost positive I saw one of those machines there."

"I think so, but I can't remember for sure," Wilf said. "I feel like I remember cows there, though. Real ones, I mean."

"I bet that machine makes a blue wax cow!" Bondi said. "Oh man, we rock. Blue cow, here we come!"

"Wait, you guys both went to the zoo? Both of you?" She looked at Bondi, who shrugged. Melissa crumpled up her napkin and tossed it at him. "Well, forget it, this one's mine, then. I'm taking the photo so I can have a fun trip to the zoo, thank you very much."

Bondi and Wilf exchanged a glance. "Sure, okay," Bondi said. "You're on cow duty. We'll work on the third clue." He turned to Wilf. "So what'd it say, anyway? You never sent me the photo."

Wilf cringed inwardly. "Oh yeah. The clue. Well, I have it. It looked *super* easy, too. But I, um . . . left it at home again. Sorry, guys."

"You don't have it, do you? You lost it." Melissa stared at him stone-faced.

Wilf laughed nervously. "No! Are you crazy? Lost? No, it's right in my room, right there on the . . . I just forgot to bring it, that's all."

Bondi looked at his watch. "Okay, well, come on. We'll go get it."

"Um, now?" Wilf swallowed hard. He was so busted.

Bondi pretended not to notice. "Yeah, why not? Melissa, meet us when you have the cow. We'll be at Wilf's. And no calling Dimitri for a ride."

"What?" Melissa scowled at him. "It'll take me three times as long without him! And he won't know anything's up, I swear."

Bondi shook his head. "Forget it, Melissa. They don't work for us; they work for Smith. We don't know if we can trust them."

Melissa rolled her eyes. "Give me a break. We can trust Dimitri."

Bondi gave her a sad smile. "We can't trust anyone. Not now. Not anymore."

To: Butler

From: Frank Jennings

Subject: Would like an update, please.

Look, I know you have a plan and everything, but none of us drivers have heard from the kids in a while. We're starting to get nervous. What's going on?

Frank

To: Frank Jennings, Inez Castillo, Dimitri Omar

From: Butler

Subject: RE: Would like an update, please.

I appreciate your concern about the children. But never fear—they'll be in touch soon. I have taken steps to move things along.

Wilf and Bondi

Wilf held the door open for Bondi. "So the clue is . . . um, in here."

"In your apartment. Yeah, you said." Bondi tossed his messenger bag so it landed with a thump in the chair by the door. He looked around like he expected the clue to come dancing over to greet them. "Okay, where is it?"

Wilf laughed. "See, that's the thing, right?"

Bondi eyed him nervously. Wilf had that crazy, twitchy look that he'd seen on cable shows. If a character in a movie had been acting like Wilf was right now, Bondi would be thinking *serial killer*. But he was pretty sure it was something else. Something worse.

"Oh no. What's the thing, Wilf? Where's the clue?"

"See, that's the thing," Wilf said again, a smile frozen on his face. He held it for a few seconds more and then cracked. "I don't know where it is," he finished in a whisper, his face white. "Don't tell Melissa. She'll kill me."

"Oh yeah, she will!" Bondi gave a short laugh. "You're a dead man unless we find that clue in the next, what, forty-five minutes? Because even if I don't tell her, she's going to notice we don't have the clue, Wilf."

"I know," Wilf said.

Bondi cracked his knuckles and looked around. "Okay, that clue's got to be here somewhere, right? Let's find that sucker and save your life."

· ·

Melissa

Melissa jogged from the bus stop to the farm area of the Lincoln Park Zoo and then screeched to a stop. It looked like there were two barns there, maybe even three. "Geez, guys, way to narrow it down."

There was no time to waste. After hesitating for only a

second, Melissa took off toward the Dairy Barn, because nothing says cow like the word *dairy*. (Well, except for the word *cow*.) The cows looked up hopefully as she hurried inside.

"Sorry, no time, cows. I promise to come back later, though." The brown cow closest to her turned her head away in disgust.

"Oh, shoot. Sorry, guys." Melissa ran over and blew a quick kiss to each of the cows. "You guys are awesome. Love you. Gotta go."

The brown cow grunted appreciatively at Melissa and went back to her tray of grain. She wasn't one to hold a grudge.

Now, where's the thingie? Melissa said to herself, scanning the building. Aside from the cows, there wasn't much to see. There was definitely no wax cow machine in sight.

"Shoot, shoot, shoot," Melissa muttered as she headed out. She didn't know what she'd do if they'd gotten this one wrong. She crossed her fingers and made a beeline for the big red barn next door.

"Aha!" she squealed.

There, on the side of the room, was a machine with the word *Mold-A-Rama* written in brightly colored letters. A glass dome covered the top of the machine, and inside Melissa could see tubes and dials and technical-looking metal rods. And in the glowing, illuminated display window at the top of the machine sat a blue cow.

Melissa ran over, pulling her money out of her pocket. She'd brought quarters and dollar bills both—there was no way she was going to be caught short this time. She didn't even mind sacrificing her worksheet money for a good cause. As she fed the first coin into the slot, she read the slogan on the machine. NOW YOU CAN OPERATE THE AMAZING MOLD-A-RAMA. AUTOMATIC MINIATURE PLAS-TIC FACTORY.

"Shoot, it *is* plastic," Melissa muttered. She hoped that wouldn't make a difference. Plastic or not, it was the clos-est to a blue wax cow they were going to get. And besides, she'd already invested a quarter. She just hoped it wasn't a trick.

Melissa finished feeding the coins into the machine and then watched while it sculpted a little blue cow. It smelled good, like crayons or something, and was still really warm when it came out of the slot.

"Blue cow, you are solution number two," she said, kiss-ing it on the head. She put it on top of the machine and took a few photos from different angles before tucking Wilf's camera carefully into her book bag. She hoped the photos would be good enough. She didn't really want to hand this little guy over to Smith—she'd kind of like to hang on to him herself. Besides, what would Mr. Smith do with a blue wax cow? (Okay, plastic. Whatever.)

Melissa checked her watch. Not bad. If she was lucky, Wilf and Bondi would have gotten a good start on the third clue, and they could go ahead and set up Wilf's meeting. Heck, if she was really lucky, they'd have solved it. Dodging a wandering toddler, Melissa double crossed her fingers and hurried to the bus.

Wilf

Wilf's mother knocked on the door to his room and
stuck her head in. Wilf was sitting in the middle of the
floor with his head in his hands, and his friend from school
was at the desk, seated backwards with his chin propped
on the back of the chair. If Wilf's mother didn't know any
better, she'd say they looked depressed. They certainly had
made a mess. There were clothes and papers thrown everywhere, the trash can had been dumped out, and the sheets
had been stripped off the bed.

She made a harrumphing noise. Wilf didn't respond.

"Wilf? Hon? Are you two having fun?"

"Oh yeah. Good times, Mom," Wilf said without looking up.

"Mmm-hmm." Wilf's mom looked at his closet, which
seemed to have vomited its contents out into the room. She
was glad to see Wilf bringing friends home, but she'd been

thinking more along the lines of board games and snacks, not full-scale destruction. "I can see. Well, I'm going downstairs to the laundry room if you need me."

"Okay."

"Anything else you need me to wash?"

"Nope. I'm good."

Wilf's mom waited, but he didn't say anything else. "Okay, well, that's where I'll be. You emptied your pockets, didn't you? Remember, I'm not doing it for you anymore, Wilf. You need to take responsibility for your things." She hated to bring it up in front of his school friend, but she was already showing incredible restraint by not mentioning the state of his room. She had her limits.

"Yeah," Wilf said, his voice muffled by his arms. "Responsibility."

"Okay, hon." She turned around and headed out. "There are cookies on the counter if you want them later," she called back over her shoulder.

Wilf snorted. Cookies. He wouldn't need any cookies. Not anymore. Because as soon as Melissa got there, he'd be dead.

Melissa, Wilf, and Bondi

Melissa stepped through the apartment's front door and peeked around. "Hellooo?"

She checked the address on the piece of paper again. The door had been open a crack, so it wasn't like she was breaking in. "Wilf?"

"In here." Bondi's voice came from a room down the hall.

Melissa pulled the cow out of her book bag and held him out in front of her like an offering.

"Looook what I have!" she sang, stepping into the room. Her grin disappeared. "Geez, guys, what happened to you?"

The room looked like a tornado had hit it and Bondi and Wilf were two of the casualties. They were flopped over the furniture like rag dolls. Melissa had a feeling it was going to take more than a blue wax cow to perk them up.

"Blue wax cow?" she said, softly this time, wiggling it in the air.

"That's great, Melissa," Bondi said. "But I think Wilf has something he wants to tell you."

Melissa dropped her arm. "You lost the clue, didn't you."

"We looked *everywhere*!" Wilf said. "Ask Bondi. It's just not here! Maybe they only gave me two?" Even as he said it, Wilf knew it wasn't true. He remembered having three clues. He even remembered not reading one of them. He just didn't remember what he'd done with it.

Melissa put her cow on the desk and looked around slowly. "Well, it has to be here. Was the room like this when you got here, Bondi?"

"Oh no, we had to work to get it like this," Bondi said, nudging a pair of stray gym shorts with his shoe. "We can't find it."

Melissa chewed her lip thoughtfully. "Okay. Could you have left it in the car?"

Wilf thought. It was definitely a possibility. But no, it didn't make sense. "Frank would've said something. He would've noticed and pointed it out to me. He was helping, remember?"

Melissa nodded. "Okay. Could you have dropped it outside sometime?"

Wilf blushed. He really didn't want to mention his day of puking. "It's possible," he finally said. He could have dropped everything he owned on puking day and never known it.

Melissa threw down her book bag. "Well, that's it, then. We're done. Guess you're heading to the Taj Mahal at three, Bondi, and I'll go to the Pope's house and hang around all Monday, since those are the only clues we have left. Hope these debit cards work for airline tickets." She gave a choked sounding laugh and stared at the floor.

Wilf and Bondi didn't say a thing. The only sound was a faucet dripping somewhere down the hall.

Finally Wilf sniffed. "Have a cookie," he said, his voice flat. "My mom got them. They're on the counter."

"Sure, okay." Melissa turned around and plodded to the kitchen. She never turned down a free cookie. Bondi and Wilf trailed behind her.

"Is your mom here?" Melissa asked as she picked up a cookie.

"She's downstairs," Wilf said, taking milk out of the refrigerator. "Laundry room. She should be back soon, though."

"Hope you emptied out your pockets, Wilf," Bondi said in his best mom voice. He took a cookie and turned to Melissa. "She seemed pretty hard core about that. Wilf needs to take responsibility."

Wilf sniffed. "Yeah, responsibility. Who cares? What difference does it make?"

"Pockets . . ." Melissa slowly lowered the cookie from her mouth. *"Did* you empty your pockets, Wilf?"

Wilf stared at her.

"How long has she been down there?" Melissa had a look of horror on her face, and when Wilf looked at Bondi, Bondi had one, too.

"A while. She should be back soo—" Suddenly it hit Wilf like a punch in the stomach. "Oh man, my pockets!"

Melissa threw her cookie back onto the plate and ran out of the apartment. "Which way? Where's the laundry room?"

Wilf shot past her and jumped down the stairs in two bounds. "Basement! Hurry!"

"It's going to be too late," Bondi said, racing after them. "She's been down there half an hour!" One of those clues would be pulp in ten minutes, never mind half an hour.

Wilf raced down the long painted cinder-block hallway in the basement and threw himself against the laundry room door, bursting in with Melissa and Bondi tumbling in behind him.

Wilf's mother was sitting on a plastic chair next to a line of spinning washers, a ratty paperback novel in her hand. "Wilf? Hon, what's wrong?"

"Laundry? Done yet?" Wilf gasped.

His mother gave him a look like he'd gone crazy. "Not even started. The washers are all full. They should be done in just a sec, though. Why?"

Wilf grinned. "Forgot to empty my pockets."

Wilf, Bondi, and Melissa

Beloved co-editor in charge of the moon.

"Come *on*!" Wilf said, slamming his book shut. "The *moon*? How can you even *pretend* this is a real thing?"

After they'd rescued the third clue from Wilf's pants, they'd headed to the library to try to solve it. But so far they hadn't been able to find the link between Chicago and the moon, let alone who the moon's editor was.

"It's a real thing," Bondi said, taking the clue out of Wilf's hand and examining it. "We just have to figure out how."

"*The moon?*"

"Hey, my clue told me to have ice cream in 1910, and I managed to do it," Melissa said. "At least the moon isn't in the past."

"You had ice cream in 1910?" Bondi said, blinking twice. Suddenly his clues seemed a lot less difficult.

"Maybe I'll take you sometime," Melissa said, shrugging.

"Do you not hear how crazy this is?" Wilf sat up and stared at them.

Bondi put down the clue and sighed. "Look, Wilf, you know what? Don't worry about it. Me and Melissa, we can figure this all out and just tell you what to say at your meeting. How's that sound?"

"Well, no, I'm not saying—" Wilf sputtered.

"Yeah, that would work," Melissa said. "You could even still go around with Frank and do whatever to keep them from suspecting. Sound good?"

Wilf gaped at them. "*No!* No way. This is my clue. My responsibility, not yours. Give me that." He snatched the slip of paper away and held it close to his chest while he looked at it, like he expected Bondi or Melissa to fight him for it. "Okay, so this is what I figure. This could be a clue about a real editor of something called the *Moon*. Is there a magazine or something called that? Or maybe this is a moon thing and the editor stuff is bonus. Right? So that's what we need to figure out."

Bondi grinned at Wilf. "Well, shoot, we need to threaten your clues more often! Next thing you know, you'll be emptying your own pockets." He turned to Melissa. "You hear that? *Moon* magazine. Sounds like a plan."

Melissa scooted her chair back up to the library computer and started typing. Technically, her time to use it had already run out, but so far she'd managed to hang on to it by glaring at everyone who came her way. "Okay, so *magazine called the Moon* . . . Nope. Nothing."

Bondi whistled. "Wow, that doesn't seem right."

Melissa pointed at the screen. "No, see? There's a bar with the word *moon* in its name, and a restaurant, but nothing that would have an editor."

Bondi leaned back in his chair. "No, I'm sure it's true. But I mean, what the what? There's nothing?" He made a face at Melissa.

Melissa scanned the page online. "Yeah, I'm not spotting any obvious Chicago moon editors at all. Maybe it's something small, though."

Wilf shook his head. "Forget the editor stuff. Focus on the moon thing. How about those moon-landing guys? The astronauts."

Melissa typed quickly and peered at the screen again. "Okay, Armstrong was an Ohio guy, Buzz Aldrin is a New Jersey guy, and this Collins guy . . . sheesh, it looks like he lived everywhere *but* Chicago. So no good there."

Wilf looked deflated. "Well, I tried."

Bondi elbowed him in the ribs. "We'll get it. We've still got time."

Melissa looked at her watch. "I don't. It's almost Gran's

McDonald's time. We'll figure it out, though. Something moon. It's got to be obvious."

"Right." Bondi patted the books. "Wilf and I will stay here and figure it out."

Wilf wilted. "We will?"

Bondi elbowed him again. "Come on, it'll be a cinch. We're practically there! Moon something, right?"

"Right," Wilf said sadly.

Melissa grinned at Bondi and headed home on the bus.

Melissa had just gotten the door unlocked when the phone in her pocket started ringing. She hurried inside, dumping her book bag and answering quickly, hardly even acknowledging Liam, who was standing in the entryway holding a newspaper.

"Hello?" Melissa said quietly. She could hear her grandmother bustling around in the living room.

"We figured it out," Bondi said breathlessly. "It's a moon rock. There used to be one at the Tribune Tower, that newspaper building on Michigan Avenue. The *Chicago Tribune* had its offices there, and it had two super-famous co-editors back in the day. They were gone by the time the Tribune Tower got the moon rock, but it was their program that got it there, so it's got to be one of them, right?"

Melissa nodded and made a face at Liam, who was still

just standing with the newspaper, not saying anything. It was weird.

What? she mouthed silently.

Liam held up the paper so that Melissa could read the headline. She stared at it, then looked up at him. He nodded slowly.

"Melissa? Melissa?" Bondi's voice sounded tiny coming out of the phone now dangling in her hand. She lifted it back up to her ear.

"Melissa, did you hear me?" He sounded irritated. "We know the answer to the third clue. We figured it out."

She took the newspaper from Liam. "That's great. I figured it out, too."

"What are you talking about?"

"Liam just showed me a newspaper article. I know what's going on. I know what the clues are for."

ECCENTRIC MILLIONAIRE'S FINAL PRANK?

Heirs forced to compete for inheritance

by Nasira Mondello

CHICAGO Since the death of eccentric multi-millionaire Enoch Ambrose, the executors of his will have been strangely quiet about the terms and even about who will inherit the vast fortune Ambrose left behind, rumored to be in the hundreds of millions of dollars. We now may know the reason why.

According to an anonymous inside source, Enoch Ambrose's will states that, in order to inherit, the millionaire's children, Linus Ambrose and Sybil Ambrose-Murgeston, both of Chicago, must compete with each other, pitting one heir against another in a twisted, winner-takes-all competition.

Attorneys at Hughes, Hughes & Hughes, longtime lawyers for Enoch Ambrose, refused to confirm or deny the existence of such a requirement.

Exactly what this competition may involve is still unknown, but when asked about this rumor, Sybil Ambrose-Murgeston had no comment except to tell this reporter to "cram it down your piehole."

Sybil Ambrose-Murgeston

Mr. Linus Ambrose
1600 N. Astor Street
Chicago, IL

My dear brother,

Anonymous leaks to the press? I would have thought such a thing beneath even you. But you continue to astonish me with the depths to which you are willing to sink. Pig.

Your loving sister,

Sybil

Linus Ambrose

Ms. Sybil Ambrose-Murgeston
1601 N. Astor Street
Chicago, IL

Dearest Sybil,

   Accusations? Again? I had nothing to do with
those anonymous leaks. It looks to me as though
the only one speaking to the press has been you.
Perhaps you should, what was that charming turn
of phrase? Oh yes. Cram it down your piehole.

                                        Yours,

                                        Linus

Melissa, Bondi, and Wilf

Melissa slapped the newspaper on the table in front of Bondi and Wilf. She'd had to wait until her grand-mother got back before she could meet them at the coffee shop, and it felt like years since Melissa had told them the news over the phone. "Voilà. How much you want to bet this little competition involves clues?"

Wilf unfolded the paper and read the article, then passed it over to Bondi.

"Sounds like that ten thousand dollars was just pocket change," Bondi said, shaking his head.

"We just handed Smith the prize," Melissa said, prop-ping her chin in her hands angrily. "We did all that work, and gave him all the answers, for practically nothing."

"Not exactly," Bondi said, his eyes gleaming. "We gave him five right answers and one wrong answer. And there are still three answers that we haven't given him yet."

Melissa raised her eyebrow. "Are we still going to? Even though we know that it's a con?"

"Sure, why not," Bondi said. "Right, Wilf?"

Wilf shrugged. "I guess." He frowned. "Actually, why would we?"

"Because, don't you see? It's our chance!" Bondi said, jumping up. "We hold all the cards now. It's our chance to show them they can't get away with it. I don't know what we'll do exactly, but we have to show them that they can't just treat us like we're stupid kids."

Melissa nodded slowly. "They think they can con us. We'll show them who the *real* suckers are . . . somehow. Right?"

"It won't get us the prize, though, will it?" Wilf said, looking from Melissa to Bondi.

"Well, no," Melissa said, dropping her chin back onto her hands.

"Okay, that stinks," Wilf said thoughtfully. "But Bondi's right. We should do it, anyway. We should do *something*. Show them who's boss. Right?" He held up his hand for a high five. Bondi and Melissa both jumped up to smack it, more or less successfully.

Melissa's eyes gleamed. "We'll think of some way to get back at Smith . . . I mean, Linus . . . I mean . . . Shoot, I don't even know what to call him anymore!" She flopped back down into the chair.

"I like Jerkface myself." Wilf snickered.

"Or Weaselbreath," Melissa said with an evil grin.

Bondi burst out laughing. "Scum-sucking pig!"

"That's still better than *Linus*." Melissa giggled.

"But, no, seriously," Wilf said, suddenly growing quiet. "We should just call him Smith. You know me—if we start calling him Linus in private, the first thing I'll do is accidentally slip up and give us away. So I say we stay with Smith."

Bondi nodded, wiping his eyes. "You're right. *Linus* feels weird, anyway. So that's settled—we'll come up with an awesome plan and then we'll come out of nowhere and take him by surprise."

"The jerk won't know what hit him," Melissa smirked.

"Besides, we might as well, since we pretty much figured out that last clue," Bondi said. "We know it's that Tribune Tower moon rock with the two editors."

Wilf nodded. "Colonel Robert McCormick and his cousin, Captain Joseph Patterson. They ran the paper together."

Melissa sat straight up. "Him! That first one! I bet it's Colonel McCormick."

"Okaaay," Bondi said, exchanging a freaked-out look with Wilf. Melissa had suddenly switched into overdrive. "Any particular reason why?"

"You know I've been watching that Ambrose documentary with my grandmother, right? Well, they mention

Colonel McCormick all the time. Apparently, Ambrose was constantly playing pranks on him when McCormick was old. I don't think they liked each other one bit."

Bondi nodded. "Then it's probably him. So we get a photo of the tower, set up a meeting, and then see what Wilf's invite says. See if Butler gives him the invitation on the sly, like he did with us. Because I'm not entirely sure Smith even knows about those."

Melissa frowned. "Yeah, it *was* just Butler. That's weird, isn't it?"

Bondi nodded. "Seems weird to me. But we don't have anything to lose at this point."

"Except handing him three more right answers," Wilf grumbled.

Bondi grinned. "That's the thing. We'll give him three answers, sure. We just aren't going to give him three more *right* answers. We're only going to give him two."

To: Inez Castillo, Dimitri Omar
From: Frank Jennings
Subject: WHOOOHOOO!!

HOT DIGGITY DOG! MY KID FIGURED OUT HIS CLUES!
Meeting with Smith tomorrow. Told you he was just a
slow starter!

To: Frank Jennings, Inez Castillo
From: Dimitri Omar
Subject: RE: WHOOOHOOO!!

You heard from your kid? Has he seen my kid? I have
not heard from her still.

To: Frank Jennings, Dimitri Omar
From: Inez Castillo
Subject: RE: WHOOOHOOO!!

Big whoop, Frank, your kid came in third. My kid is
still the winner of the big prize. And no, no one's heard
from your kid, Dimitri. Give it a rest.

Wilf

Wilf's leg jiggled nervously while Smith flipped through his photos. The plan had seemed like a good one when they'd all come up with it. *Fake him out completely,* they said. *Don't just give him a wrong answer, give him a REALLY wrong answer,* they said. *One so wrong that he'll have to say something—if he knows it's wrong, that is.* Sure, that had seemed great at the time. And Wilf had been psyched that he'd be playing the most important part. But now that he was actually doing it, Wilf had a feeling Smith wouldn't like being tricked, and he sure didn't want to be around if Smith figured out what they were doing.

Mr. Smith held up the first photo, of the *Bowman* and *Spearman* statues on Congress Avenue. "The clue gave you two Bible verses. And you came up with this as the answer?" Smith made it sound like that was the stupidest thing anyone had ever said.

Wilf swallowed hard. He *knew* this one was right. "Yes. Because Jeremiah 6:23 refers to their bow and spear, and Psalm 46:9 says the bow and spear have been broken. And those two statues, you'll notice they don't have any weapons—but if they did, they would be a bow and a spear. 'Cause they're called Bowman and Spearman. It's not like they'd have an Uzi or a rocket launcher or something, right?" Wilf gave a hollow laugh and then stared down at the floor. He needed to get out of here before he made a total fool of himself.

"Very good," Smith barked, slapping the photo onto the desk. "Now this one: *Beloved co-editor in charge of the moon?*"

"Right, so, um . . . the Tribune Tower? Used to have a moon rock. So the editor would be Colonel McCormick. Since he was in charge, along with his cousin, Captain Patterson."

Mr. Smith glared at Wilf with narrowed eyes. "That one seems almost too easy."

"Yeah, well." Wilf forced himself to laugh, shrugging. "Maybe for you, 'cause you're . . . so . . . smart . . . and all." Wilf bit the inside of his cheek. Another dumb response. If there was one thing Wilf didn't like, it was high-pressure situations. But he had to do his part. He couldn't let Melissa and Bondi down.

Mr. Smith's eyes narrowed even more. "Exactly," he

finally said. He picked up the third photo. "And this third solution?"

Wilf tried to keep his voice calm. "So that one is about Madame Tussaud and Mrs. O'Leary's little blue friend, right? It's pretty obvious it's a blue cow. So the answer has to be the, uh . . ." Wilf took a deep breath. "The Blue Cow Cafe on Michigan Avenue."

A small, strangled noise came from the far side of the room. Out of the corner of his eye, Wilf could see Butler fold his arms over his chest and cover his mouth with one hand. But Butler didn't say a word.

"So that's the answer. Blue Cow Cafe," Wilf repeated. "Yessir, that's it, all right." He stared at the picture in Smith's hand. The cafe *was* on Michigan Avenue—that was true—but it was the Michigan Avenue in Big Rapids, Michigan. Bondi had gotten the picture off the Internet.

Mr. Smith stared at the photo for a long moment and then stared back at Wilf. Finally, he slapped the photo down onto the desk. "Well. That's that, then."

Wilf felt frozen to the spot. "That's what, then?"

"That's the end of the competition. Well done, boy, very well done. I didn't think you had it in you." He clapped his hands together and rubbed them like he was trying to start a fire. "Congratulations. Now, turn over your game paraphernalia to Butler, and we'll be in touch about the prize. Looks like that Bondi boy may have broken a rule or two, and that Burris girl, well, she's a shifty one, but that's all yet to be determined. Butler will show you out." Smith shuffled the photos into a manila envelope on his desk and waved his hand dismissively.

Butler led Wilf out into the hallway and pressed the elevator button. "You may need your game paraphernalia a little longer, so no need to turn that over quite yet. But this is for you." He held out a small cream envelope.

Wilf took it and stuck it in his pocket. "Thanks." He'd never been so relieved in his life. He was so glad the whole thing was over.

Butler pushed the elevator button and waited silently as Wilf shifted from one foot to the other.

Wilf stared at his feet. He knew he should say something, come up with the perfect question that would bust the whole competition wide open and reveal all the Ambrose secrets. But if he said the wrong thing, he could ruin everything and blow it for all three of them. Wilf took a deep breath as the elevator got closer. He had to say something.

The elevator dinged.

"So," Wilf said as the doors opened. "Um. Go, Cubs."

Butler nodded. "Yes. Go, Cubs."

Wilf got into the elevator. He could feel his ears turning bright red.

"Blue Cow Cafe," Butler muttered under his breath as the elevator doors closed.

Wilf waited until the elevator had started going down before tearing open the envelope. He scanned the invitation quickly.

Your attendance is requested
24th Floor of the Alamo.

Wilf broke into a grin. He squeezed through the elevator doors as they started to open and jogged out to the sidewalk.

· ·

Bondi

B ondi was crouched behind a scraggly bush.
    Wilf thrust the card in his face. "Check it out, it's different. Butler *totally* gave it to me on the sly. And give me a break—twenty-fourth floor of the Alamo? I saw *Pee-wee's Big Adventure*; I know that's a scam. The Alamo doesn't have

a basement, and I'm pretty sure it doesn't have a twenty-fourth floor, either."

Bondi nodded. He'd seen *Pee-wee's Big Adventure*, too. "And what about Smith? He didn't know it was the wrong answer?"

Wilf grinned. "Not a clue. I think Butler knew, but Smith didn't know a thing. Weird, huh?"

"Yeah, weird." Bondi peered around the corner. He could see a familiar black car idling just down the block. "Frank's here. You'd better hustle, or he's going to notice something's up."

Wilf slung his backpack over his shoulder. "You'll meet us when you get done tailing Smith?"

Bondi nodded. "Oh yeah. Now get, before they spot us!" He crouched back behind the bush and tried to act inconspicuous.

Wilf gave him the okay sign and sauntered over to Frank's car.

Bondi watched as Wilf high-fived Frank and they drove away, and then he turned his attention back to the door. He had one last chance to follow Smith, and he wasn't going to blow it. Not this time.

• •

Things to Remember the Next Time You Hide Under a Bush

by Bondi Johnson

1. Warm up with some deep knee bends so you can squat for a long period of time. Squatting is essential for hiding behind a bush.

2. Try to pick a big, full bush, and not a scrawny one.

3. Try not to freak out when something touches your neck. It's probably not a bug.

4. Not a big one, anyway.

5. Oh God, it's a bug. Have alternate hiding location in mind for when a ginormous bloodsucking insect crawls down your collar and you abandon your original bush.

• •

Bondi shook out his jacket and tried to blend in with the less buggy–seeming bush on the other side of the doorway. It wasn't working, but he hadn't seen Smith or Butler leave, so it didn't make much of a difference, anyway. Besides, it wasn't easy pretending to be a bush.

The door to the building swung open, and Bondi immediately dropped to the ground. He peered through the leaves as the person walked down the sidewalk. Smith.

A car pulled up in front of the building as Smith got to the curb, and he quickly got inside. Alone. He slammed the door as the car pulled away, and it disappeared down the street.

Bondi hesitated, still half crouching. He hadn't figured on Smith leaving without Butler. The plan had been to tail the two of them. But he couldn't lose Smith. He was the important one in the equation, anyway, right?

Bondi straightened up a little more to get a better look. He was just leaning forward when he realized someone was behind him.

And a hand clamped down on the back of his neck.

• •

Wilf: SUCCESS! I totally pulled one over on the old man. Meet me in five.

Melissa: NOT A SECURE LINE, DOOFUS! ZIP IT! Is Bondi still doing the stakeout? I have a bad feeling about that.

Wilf: Yeah, but he'll be fine. What could happen?

Bondi

Bondi froze and tried to scream, but it came out like more of a gurgling sound. This was it. It was all over. He was a dead man.

Another hand clamped down on Bondi's shoulder and pulled him into an upright position. Bondi squeezed his eyes shut and waited for the worst to happen. He knew the bush had been a bad idea. He just didn't know it would be his last bad idea.

"Ah, Mr. Johnson. I hoped I might find you here. Taking up an interest in shrubbery, I presume?"

Bondi turned his head slightly, opened his eyes, and cringed. It was Butler.

"Not satisfied with your win?" Mr. Butler stretched his thin lips into a smile.

Bondi tried not to squirm in Butler's grip, but it was like

he was caught in a vise. He was starting to lose feeling in his shoulder. "Well, no, I mean . . ."

"Or is it something else you're not satisfied with?" Butler let go of Bondi and patted him on the arm. Not exactly the move of a killer, but there was a chance Butler was just toying with him.

"Sit?" Butler pointed to a bench a few yards away.

"Sure," Bondi said. Anything to get out from behind the bush. You don't have a lot of options when you're operating from inside shrubbery.

Mr. Butler sat down and patted the bench next to him. He stared out into the street for a couple of minutes. "I would be willing to bet you're a newspaper reader," he finally said. "Am I right, Mr. Johnson?"

Bondi sat down warily, trying to assess the situation. Butler was acting like they were shooting the breeze, not like he'd just caught him spying. Bondi cleared his throat. "That's right."

"Seen anything of interest lately?" Butler glanced at Bondi. His face was completely relaxed.

"As a matter of fact, I did," Bondi said, watching Butler carefully. "About Enoch Ambrose. Sounds like he had an interesting will."

Butler nodded somberly. "Yes, yes he did. Quite interesting. I wonder if you realize quite how interesting it is."

Bondi shifted uncomfortably. "It sounds to me," he said

slowly, "like there are clues, and whoever solves them inherits everything. Am I right?"

Mr. Butler raised his eyebrows. "Yes, I'd say that's an extremely accurate assessment."

Bondi took a deep breath and let it out in a rush. If Butler was going to take him out, Bondi might as well lay all his cards on the table. "So basically, this contest was just a scam. Melissa and Wilf and me, we were conned into helping Linus Ambrose get the inheritance. All that work—it was all for nothing."

Butler smiled. "I don't know if I'd say *that*."

Bondi scowled at him. "Oh yeah? Why not? If we got the clues right, Linus Ambrose inherits. If we didn't, his sister does. Either way, none of us will ever see any scholarship money, because 'Mr. Smith' will decide we all broke the rules. Am I right?"

Butler brushed a piece of nonexistent lint off his sleeve. "I don't know how much you know about inheritance law, Bondi, but as I was saying, this will is . . . unusual in its wording. It states that whosoever solves the clues will be the heir."

Bondi rolled his eyes. "That's what I just said."

Butler smiled slightly. "Is it?"

Bondi's eyes widened. "Wait, did you say *whosoever*?"

Butler inclined his head. "Whosoever. The terms are quite clear."

"It doesn't say that it has to be Linus or Sybil?"

Butler smiled. "The clues were given to them, that's true. And they are certainly in a very advantageous position. But the will plainly states *whosoever*. There are no restrictions in place." He eased himself to his feet and dusted off his pants. "Now, if you'll excuse me, Mr. Johnson. You have your invitation, I trust?"

Bondi nodded. He didn't trust himself to say anything.

"I suggest that you and your friends not miss that appointment. I suggest it very strongly, in fact." He bowed his head slightly and started off down the street.

Bondi stared at him as he walked away and then launched himself off the bench.

"But wait, are you for real?" Bondi asked, jogging after him. "Don't you work for Mr. Ambrose? He's going to be really mad that you told me that stuff."

Butler smiled. "My employer was and has always been Mr. *Enoch* Ambrose. And you're right, Bondi. Mr. *Linus* Ambrose would be angry, if we'd had this conversation. So it's good that we didn't."

Bondi gave a short laugh. "Right. What conversation?"

"Exactly. Best of luck to you. Don't let us down." Butler nodded solemnly, and then turned and strolled slowly away down the street.

Bondi: MEETING NOW! URGENT URGENT URGENT!

Melissa: No kidding. We've been waiting for you FOREVER.

Wilf: Any news?

Bondi: OH, THERE'S NEWS. BIG NEWS.

Melissa, Bondi, and Wilf

"So let me get this straight. There's no scholarship. We're not competing for ten thousand dollars. We're competing for *millions* of dollars?" Melissa wondered if she should pinch herself. This sure didn't seem like real life. She looked over at the doughnut counter. With a million dollars, she could buy them all. She could probably buy the whole coffee shop.

"Yep." Bondi nodded enthusiastically.

Melissa stared at him. Bondi didn't seem quite real, either, nodding like a bobblehead like that.

"And let me get this straight. We're not competing against each other. We're competing against Smith and his sister? Enoch Ambrose's kids?"

Bobblehead Bondi nodded again.

Melissa stared at him. "You must've heard wrong."

"No, it's right! It's totally right. If we can solve the clues, we inherit. We just need to figure out our invitations. Where we're supposed to go, and when. That's it."

"Oh, is that it? Well, great," Melissa said. "What a cinch." She snorted, then frowned. She didn't usually snort in dreams. But this couldn't be real. Could it?

She turned and stared at Wilf, who was just sitting like a lump staring at them both. Melissa stuck out her arm. "Wilf? Would you do me a favor?"

He looked down at her arm and seemed to understand. "You sure?"

"Please."

Wilf reached out and pinched her.

Melissa winced. "Yep, that hurt."

Wilf dug a card out of his pocket and handed it to her. "Now you do *me* a favor. Here."

Melissa took it. It was his invitation.

Wilf pointed at it. "You'd better hang on to it. 'Cause I'll lose it. You know I will."

Melissa put the card in her book bag. Wilf would totally lose it.

"If this was a dream, I wouldn't," Wilf said, watching as she zipped the bag closed. "But this is real life. Right?"

Melissa nodded again. The pinch had proved that. "Real life. Right."

Wilf slapped his hands together and rubbed them quickly in a perfect imitation of Smith. Then his face broke into a grin.

"Well, what are we waiting for? Who wants to win a million dollars?"

• •

Bondi's invitation:

Your attendance is requested
3 P.M., at the Taj Mahal.

Melissa's invitation:

Your attendance is requested
This Monday, Clementine Hall,
Pope's Residence.

Wilf's invitation:

Your attendance is requested
24th Floor of the Alamo.

• •

"Okay, so obviously the meeting isn't in India and Italy and Texas at the same time." Melissa chewed on her pencil thoughtfully.

"Obviously," Bondi said, trying not to look at her pencil. It was grossing him out.

"So we split up? We have debit cards," Wilf said. He hadn't used his card in days, and it just felt wrong, like he was wasting free money. "Do they sell airline tickets to kids?"

"That doesn't sound right," Bondi said.

"I don't think we're supposed to go to these places at all. I think they're just hints." Melissa put down her pencil. It made a spit mark on her notebook paper. "We just need to figure them out."

"Then we'll figure them out. So, Pope's Residence. A church in Chicago? An Indian church? Something like that?" Wilf shook his head. It sounded stupid as soon as he said it.

"Don't forget the Alamo," Bondi said.

"Right, the Alamo. So an Indian-Texan Catholic church? Is there one of those?" Wilf didn't think there was. He felt like he would've heard about something like that.

"Oh, please. For real?" Melissa scoffed.

"There could be!"

"Even if there was, how many churches have twenty-four

floors?" Bondi said. "We've got to get serious. This isn't that hard."

"Oh, sorry, I thought it was," Melissa snapped.

"No, it's not!" Bondi said. "Think about it. Smith didn't give us these clues. They came from *Butler*. So you know what that means."

"Smith doesn't want us at the meeting," Melissa said.

Bondi shook his head. "No."

Wilf rolled his eyes. "What, you think he *wants* us to show up?"

Bondi shot Wilf a look so cold it practically froze Wilf's nose hairs. "No, *Wilf*. Of course not. It means Linus Ambrose doesn't need us to solve these last clues. Because he already knows what they mean."

Wilf and Melissa exchanged a look.

"Well, crud," Wilf said.

• •

Inez: Okay, I've had it with this waiting stuff. It's go time.

Dimitri: Yes. I go too.

Melissa, Bondi, Wilf

Melissa bounced down the stairs of the coffee shop, followed by Bondi and Wilf. So closely, in fact, that it caused a pileup when she skidded to a stop on the front stoop.

"Melissa, what the—?" Bondi started, his voice dying away as he realized what she was looking at.

Standing in a row across the street were Dimitri, Inez, and Frank. They didn't look happy.

"Well, this is awkward," Melissa said under her breath.

"Tell me about it," Bondi said softly. "What do we do?"

"Hey, Frank, how'd you know we were all here?" Wilf shouted across the street.

Frank jerked his head toward Dimitri.

"Hey, Dimitri, how'd you know we were all here?" Wilf shouted.

Dimitri pointed at Inez.

"Hey, Inez—" Wilf started to shout.

"What, you kids think I wasn't going to use that GPS on your phones? Grow up!" Inez scowled at Wilf.

Wilf pulled out his phone and looked at it. "Oh, right. GPS. Cool."

Melissa glared at Bondi and Wilf. "Look, if we trust Butler, we can trust them, right?" she said quietly.

Bondi shrugged helplessly. "I don't know."

"But we're trusting Butler?"

Bondi made a face. "Do we have a choice?"

Melissa rolled her eyes. "Wait here."

Without another word, she marched across the deserted street. "One question, Dimitri. Okay?"

"Okay."

"Who do you work for? Who hired you? And don't say Smith, because I know his name is Ambrose."

Dimitri nodded. "That is true. Mr. Ambrose hired me."

Melissa clenched her jaw, and turned her back on him. She had just started across the street when she hesitated.

She swiveled back around. "You mean *Linus* Ambrose?"

Dimitri cocked his head, a faint smile on his lips. "This is two questions. You said one."

"Dimitri! *Linus Ambrose?*"

His smile widened. "Not Linus, no. I worked for Enoch Ambrose. The late Ambrose father."

Melissa looked at Inez and Frank. "What about you guys? Which Ambrose hired you?"

Inez gave a barky laugh. "Are you kidding me? We worked for Enoch. Those kids of his are looney tunes."

Melissa grinned. "That's all I needed to know," she said, turning around and giving two thumbs up to Wilf and Bondi.

Sunday

Bondi's invitation:

> *Your attendance is requested*
> *3 P.M., at the Taj Mahal.*

Melissa's invitation:

> *Your attendance is requested*
> *This Monday, Clementine Hall,*
> *Pope's Residence.*

Wilf's invitation:

> *Your attendance is requested*
> *24th Floor of the Alamo.*

HEY MOM,

YOU KNOW THAT SCHOOL PROJECT? I'M GOING TO BE WORKING ON IT ALL DAY. IT'S SUPER IMPORTANT. SEE YOU LATER.

THANKS,
WILF

Nice to see you taking an interest in academics! Good for you!

XOXO Mom

L,

Tell Gran I'll be gone all day.
Tell her school stuff. Even
though it's you—know—what.

M

P.S. Not a word to ANYONE.
Seriously.

P.P.S. I'll give you the scoop
when I get back. But only if you
haven't told. Not kidding.

P.P.P.S. Destroy this note. (Not
kidding here, either.)

Bondi: Working in the library today, see you guys tonight. Did you try that kale salad I whipped up?

Mom: Yes, I'm impressed! Are you taking home ec at school this year?

Bondi: HOME EC? Where do you think I go to school? 1952?

Dad: Don't tell your mother, but thank God for that kale salad. That stuff she was making was about to kill me.

Mom: Hey, I heard that!

Melissa, Bondi, and Wilf

Your attendance is requested
24th Floor of the Alamo.

Your attendance is requested
3 P.M., at the Taj Mahal.

Your attendance is requested
This Monday, Clementine Hall,
Pope's Residence.

"Putting the clues in a different order isn't going to make the answer magically appear, Bondi," Melissa said, watching him shuffle the clues into various arrangements on the library table, his tongue sticking out of the corner of his mouth.

"You never know what's going to do the trick, Melissa," Bondi said. "And, if you hadn't noticed, Monday is *tomorrow.*"

"Yeah, I know, okay? It's not my fault we're still totally in the dark about where we're supposed to go," she said, hovering over Bondi's shoulder.

"Look, we figured out the moon clue, and we'll figure out these. We're fine," Bondi said, trying to ignore Melissa's breath on the back of his neck. If she didn't stop hovering soon, he was going to have to do something serious. Like stand up or something.

Wilf snickered across the room. He'd draped himself over one of the reading room chairs and was flipping through an *Encyclopedia Britannica*—volume 5, *Chile–Czech*. His theory was that the answer had to be in there somewhere, so he was going to go through volume by volume until he found it. "Yeah, I don't even know how we managed that one, though. Seriously, moon rock?"

Bondi forced himself to stay cool and collected. Just focus on the clues, even if those two were acting like idiots and holding him back. "Well, we did. We'll get this one, too. We just need to try everything."

"And the thing is, it's not even at the Tribune Tower anymore!" Wilf laughed. "It's like the only thing that's missing. You wouldn't believe all the stuff that place has, all stuck in it. It's crazy!" He slapped volume 5, *Chile–Czech*, down on the table in favor of volume 9, *G–Gyro*.

"Wait, what? It has stuff *stuck in it*?" Melissa asked, straightening up.

"Yeah," Bondi said, relieved to have airspace over his shoulder again. "Embedded in the outside. Well, not the moon rock—that was in a window display. But it has artifacts from all over."

Wilf flopped back in his seat. "It was part of a program that McCormick guy set up—he had Tribune reporters bring things back from all over the world, and then he stuck them in the outside of the building. You know, fragments from famous buildings or whatever."

Melissa almost didn't want to breathe. "Famous buildings like what? Like . . . the Alamo?"

Bondi straightened up so fast that if Melissa had still been hovering he would've knocked her cold. "Oh man. Oh man, oh man, oh man. There's a list. Of the stuff, the artifacts. *Where did we put the list, Wilf?*"

Wilf dropped volume 9 and scrambled for his notebook. "Beats me. I thought you had it!"

Bondi yanked a crumpled printout out of the back of his notebook. "Oh man. Oh man. Okay . . . Alamo, Alamo, Alamo." He moved his finger slowly down the list. "There are something like a hundred of them," he said, glancing up at Melissa apologetically. "Okay, *Alamo!* It's there. There's a piece of the Alamo at the Tribune Tower."

Melissa picked up the next invitation. "Okay, try Clementine Hall. Pope's residence."

"Okay. Pope, pope, pope, pope, pope . . ." Bondi

muttered, going through the list again. His eyes grew wide. "Got it. It's there! The pope's residence is there!"

Melissa's fists were clenched so hard her knuckles were white. "What's the last one? Wilf?"

"Taj Mahal," Wilf said. "Taj Mahal's the last one."

Bondi went down through the list again, and his face broke into an enormous smile. "Right there!" he said, jabbing the list with his finger. "Taj Mahal!"

"It's the Tribune Tower," Melissa squealed, clapping her hand over her mouth when she realized how loud she'd done it. "Tribune Tower! That's where we go!"

"Tribune Tower, twenty-fourth floor," Bondi grinned, fist-bumping Wilf and Melissa. "Monday at three P.M. We are set."

· ·

Wilf: Come pick us up. We're going to be millionaires!

· ·

Frank was the only driver waiting when Bondi, Wilf, and Melissa raced down the library steps, clues and invitations carefully packed away in Melissa's book bag.

"What the heck? Where are the others?" Bondi said, skidding to a stop in front of Frank's car. He looked up and down the street, but no Inez or Dimitri.

"Coffee shop down the street. How's hot chocolate sound?" Frank smiled, but the smile didn't reach his eyes.

"Well, okay," Melissa said, looking at Frank suspiciously. She knew a fake smile when she saw one. "But why?"

Frank shrugged. "We wondered if you'd let us take a peek at the clues. Old Ambrose could be pretty sneaky. We just want to see if we can spot any of his . . . pranks."

"You think it's a trick," Wilf said flatly.

"Not necessarily. But there might be a little . . . *twist* in there," Frank said apologetically.

"I guess that'd be okay," Bondi said slowly. "We're doing fine without your help, though."

"I know. I know you are," Frank said, starting down the street. "I'd just hate for Linus to get the better of you."

. . . .

Dimitri was setting a large plate of cookies on the table as they came into the coffee shop. Melissa slid into the booth and grabbed a cookie, holding it with her teeth as she unzipped her book bag and retrieved the clue packet.

She pushed it toward Dimitri. "This has all the clues— you know about those. We each got three to solve. And then these last three cards are invitations to a meeting place, but you need all three to figure it out. We just solved that one—it's the Tribune Tower," she said, biting into her cookie. "We're supposed to go there with the answers to the other clues."

Inez pulled out the envelope of clue slips and thumbed through them while Dimitri started reading the instruction sheets.

"That sounds . . . pretty straightforward," Frank said slowly.

"*Too* straightforward," Inez said. "Nothing Enoch Ambrose did was straightforward. There's no way that's all there is to it."

Wilf groaned. "For real, guys? No offense, but just because we figured it out ourselves doesn't mean it's wrong."

"Ashtray?" Inez said, pulling out her shoulder bag and scanning the table.

"No smoking," Dimitri said quietly.

"Great." Inez threw her cigarettes back into her bag. "You're sure you got the meeting place right?"

"Oh yeah," Melissa said.

"Positive," Wilf said.

"One hundred percent," Bondi said.

"And you're sure you've got the clue answers right?"

"Oh yeah," Melissa said.

"Positive," Wilf said.

"Ninety-eight percent," Bondi said.

Inez raised an eyebrow. "Ninety-eight percent?"

"We're pretty sure," Bondi said. "Almost one hundred percent. But who knows?"

"Probably closer to ninety-nine point forty-four percent," Melissa said.

"Like the soap," Wilf said.

Frank, Dimitri, and Inez all looked over the table at Wilf.

"You know. The soap? Ivory?" Wilf said, squirming a little in his seat. He picked up a cookie and stuck it in his mouth. It wasn't his fault if they were ignorant about pop culture.

Inez sighed. "Well, all I have to say is you better have those answers down cold."

"We will," Bondi said.

"Because there's no telling what old Ambrose stuck in that will of his. You didn't know him. He was a trickster. There was nothing he liked more than pulling a fast one."

"We'll be ready," Bondi said. "Right, guys?" He raised his hand for a high five. Melissa and Wilf responded, with varying degrees of success.

"Excuse me." Dimitri put one of the papers from the packet onto the table. "What is this, please?"

"What is what?" Bondi leaned forward, frowning.

Dimitri picked up the page and read it out loud. "'Always remember: One points you forward. One takes you back. One is a trick.'"

"Oh crud," Wilf said.

"I forgot about that part," Bondi said with a groan.

Melissa put the rest of her cookie down uneaten.

Inez took the paper from Dimitri and peered at it closely. "That's Enoch Ambrose's handwriting."

Dimitri nodded. "These other pages, the contract with rules for you—I think they are from Mr. Linus. But this page is not."

"So whatever this is about, it's definitely part of the inheritance?" Wilf slumped back in the booth.

"So it would appear," Dimitri said.

Bondi crammed the last cookie in his mouth. "Snack time's over," he said once he'd finished chewing. "We've got more work to do."

· ·

PLAN OF ATTACK:

Melissa–Find out everything there is to know about the
Tribune Tower, 24th floor specifically.

Wilf–Look up info about Enoch Ambrose's pranks.

Bondi–Double-check clue answers to make sure they're right.

EVERYONE–Figure out which of your clues points you
forward, which one takes you back, and which one is a
trick. Also, figure out what the heck that means.

RECONVENE–Tomorrow, coffee shop, 10 A.M. (Forget
school. School is out.)

Frank, Inez, and Dimitri–Provide snacks.

DEADLINE–3 P.M. tomorrow, nonnegotiable

Monday

TRIBUNE TOWER
MONDAY, 3 P.M.
24TH FLOOR

ATTN: Morton Middle School Office

Melissa Burris will be out today. She's got scholarship obligations that are confidential and secret, and she needs to focus on them so she won't embarrass the school. You understand.

Signed,
Melissa's grandmother

To: Office Staff, Noyes Central:

Bondi Johnson will be out today. He's either coming down with something really contagious or he has a kale allergy. We're keeping him under observation.

Signed,
Bondi's mother

To Whom It May Concern at Sutherland
Academy:

Wilf will be out today. His grandmother
died. Not the one that died before, the
other one.

Signed,
Wilf's mother

Melissa, Wilf, Bondi

"I don't know how convincing our excuse notes were," Melissa said, dumping her book bag on the coffee shop chair. "We should've tried to make them sound more realistic."

Wilf shrugged. "What are they going to do? If they have a problem with it, we'll just give them, like, ten thousand dollars, and I bet they shut up then."

"Sure, but first we have to *win* the money," Melissa said. "Did you guys find anything cool? There is a *lot* of crazy stuff about the twenty-fourth floor of the Tribune Tower. Like, super weird."

"Weird how?" Bondi came over to the table with a muffin almost as big as his head.

"Weird like secret-rooms-and-hidden-doors weird. That kind of weird." Melissa eyed Bondi's muffin.

"Wait, hidden doors? In a corporate building? The Tribune Tower is where the newspaper offices were. Come on." Bondi pulled his muffin a little closer. He didn't like the way Melissa was looking at it.

"Well, it's true. And I have proof." Melissa hesitated. "I'll show you if you give me part of that muffin."

Bondi groaned. He should've known he'd never manage to keep that muffin for himself. He pushed his plate into the middle of the table.

Melissa grinned and tore the muffin in half, daintily putting her half onto a napkin in front of her. Then she reached into her book bag and pulled out a book.

"You are not going to believe this," she said.

"'The Chicago Tribune Tower Competition'?" Wilf craned his neck to read the title. "You're right, I don't believe it. What does that have to do with anything? That had to be a million years ago."

"Because it's got this." Melissa opened the book and pushed it toward them, carefully avoiding the muffin plate. "See that? That's a map, my friend. Of the twenty-fourth floor."

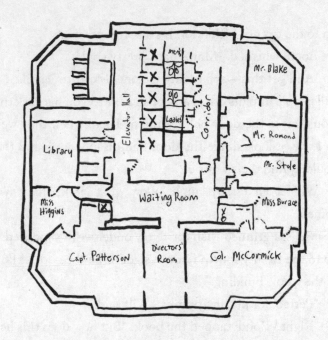

Bondi and Wilf leaned forward and inspected the floor plan. "That's where we're going?" Wilf said.

"And it's all laid out for us, just like that?" Bondi was impressed.

Melissa nodded. "Just like that. Right there, you see Captain Patterson's and Colonel McCormick's offices? Well, according to this book, they're mirror images of one another. And the walls in those offices are covered with wooden panels and have hidden closets, doorways, and even two secret stairways. There are pictures on the next page. But look here." She pointed at the bottom of the map. "That's where each office has a hidden staircase that goes up to the twenty-fifth floor. It's a secret escape."

Bondi whistled. "Man, that's pretty cool."

"And get this—apparently Colonel McCormick liked to call people into his office and push a button on his desk that would close the door behind them. Then, when they went to leave, it looked like the door had disappeared, and they couldn't find their way out."

Wilf let out a sharp laugh. "Wow, what a jerk! That's awesome!"

Melissa grinned. "Isn't it? No wonder we're supposed to go to the twenty-fourth floor. It's got to be the coolest floor in the whole building."

"Perfect for playing pranks," Wilf said.

"Right." Bondi tapped the book. "But how does this help us with the clues?"

Melissa's face fell. "Well, beats me. But I figured this is all good to know, right? We can at least know what we're getting into when we go up there."

"Yeah, I guess . . ." Bondi said doubtfully. He looked at the clock on his phone. They only had a few hours left, and it felt like there was still too much they weren't sure about. "Well, I looked at all the clues last night, and I think they're all right. I mean, they look right to me."

Melissa took a bite of muffin and nodded solemnly. "We can't afford to mess any of those up."

"Nope." Bondi pushed his piece of muffin back into the

middle of the table. He'd lost his appetite. "What'd you find out about Ambrose and McCormick, Wilf? Anything helpful?"

Wilf shook his head. "Not a ton. They didn't like each other, that was for sure. And Ambrose pulled a couple of good ones on McCormick. Apparently, McCormick was really afraid the US was going to be invaded through Canada, and one time Ambrose made him think Canadian troops were gathering on the border. I got that much."

Bondi slumped back into his chair. "So not a ton."

"Well, no. Like I said."

Bondi was starting to wish he hadn't eaten any of the muffin at all. "And this other stuff? The *points you forward, takes you back* stuff?" No one said anything. He sighed heavily. "I'll admit, I had trouble there. All I could figure was that the fountain was the trick, since it fooled me. And I guess the Skydeck Ledge points you forward? Since it's new? And that would make the Rookery the one that takes you back."

"Why?" Melissa pulled Bondi's leftover muffin closer to her. He didn't react.

"Because it's old? It's lame, but it's all I've got."

Melissa casually transferred the muffin to her napkin. "Yeah, I don't know about these. For mine, I figure the *Contribution* frieze points you forward, since it's the first of the three friezes, and then the death statue is the trick, because it totally was. And maybe the ice cream and baby chicks take you back, because they're from 1910? And, you know . . . babies," Melissa finished lamely.

"Sure, okay, I guess," Bondi said unhappily. It was all too much. "Is this even what we're supposed to be doing?"

"I don't know." Melissa frowned, crumbling the muffin into little bits. She stared at the mess she'd made and pushed it away. "We're going to lose, aren't we?" she said finally.

"*No!*" Wilf said, slapping his hand down on the table. It was a bad idea, because he caught the edge of Melissa's book and bruised his pinky finger. But he didn't care. "We're *not* going to lose! And those sound like excellent explanations." He wasn't sure about that baby chick one, but whatever, Melissa was smart. It was probably spot-on. "Here are mine—I think the blue cow takes you back because it makes you think of the Chicago fire, which was a long time ago. And the warriors, they're pointing you forward? Since they're on horses, so that's transportation? And then the moon rock is the trick, since some people think the moon landing was a hoax. See? Am I right? We're golden!"

He put his hand up for a high five. "Right?" he said weakly. Finally he put his hand down. "Oh man. We're going to get slaughtered in there."

To: Wilf Samson
From: Bob Bukowski
Subject: Sorry, also Homework

Hey Wilf,
Chad in the office asked me to get your homework
assignments to you, so give me a call when you get
home and I'll tell you what you need to do. I'm real
sorry about your grandmother—that really stinks.

See you later,
Bob (from third period)

P.S. How many grandmothers do you have, anyway?

To: Melissa Burris
From: Tanisha Cole
Subject: You better HIDE

Melissa, where are you? Mrs. Orlin is on a RAMPAGE.
What the heck did you do to her? She called me
into the office and grilled me for TWO CLASS
PERIODS about where you were, what you're up to,

EVERYTHING. And that scholarship excuse isn't going to fly anymore—she knows it's a scam. Their website has been taken down and the phone's disconnected and she is MAD AS ALL GET OUT.

Watch yourself,
Tanisha

To: Bondi Johnson
From: Jamal Jones
Subject: RIP Kale

Bondi, buddy, is it true you're in the hospital because you're allergic to kale? That's what Mrs. Gray in the office is telling everybody, and they're talking about making the school a kale-free zone. (Thanks for that, by the way.)

Peace,
Jamal

To: Melissa Burris
From: Judy Orlin
Subject: Disciplinary action imminent.

Miss Burris:
I don't know what kind of game you're playing, but your little con is over. I know you rigged this whole "scholarship" in order to skip school, and don't think I'm going to let you get away with it.

It has become obvious to all of us in the administrative office that Morton Middle School is not equipped to deal with your behavioral issues and troubled home life and "acting out." Therefore, when you see fit to return to school, we will immediately take steps to relocate you to a more appropriate educational facility, perhaps of the boarding or military variety.

Best,
Mrs. Judy Orlin
Guidance Counselor

Melissa, Bondi, Wilf

"Well, here goes nothing, right?" Melissa craned her neck to look up at the Tribune Tower.

They'd found the pieces of the Alamo, Taj Mahal, and Papal Residence embedded in the walls, and taken photos in case they needed to prove that they'd found them. Even though just being at the right location pretty much proved they'd figured it out.

Melissa smiled as she saw the frieze called *Contribution* on the InterContinental Hotel building just north of the Tribune Tower. It felt like a good sign. And they definitely needed all the good signs they could get.

"How much time do we have left?" She didn't want to go in, but she didn't want to just hang around outside anymore, either.

Bondi checked his phone. "Five minutes. We should probably head up."

"Right. We should," Wilf said.

None of them moved. Bondi rolled his shoulders and tried to shake the tension out of his arms. He wasn't used to being nervous like this.

"Well?" Melissa turned around to where Dimitri, Frank, and Inez were standing. They had to do this. It would be the stupidest thing ever for them to figure out all the clues and then miss out on the prize because they'd taken too long getting upstairs. "So, thanks, guys. I guess we'll let you know."

Inez laughed. Or coughed, Melissa wasn't sure which. "Oh, no, you don't. You think we're going to miss all the fireworks?"

Dimitri smiled. "We will escort you."

Melissa felt giddy laughter rising in her chest. "Really?"

Frank nodded. "Are you kidding? We wouldn't miss it." He clapped Wilf on the back.

Melissa elbowed Bondi in the ribs. "They're coming, too." Then she punched Wilf lightly on the shoulder. "Did you hear that, Wilf?"

"I heard," Wilf said, smiling.

Bondi cracked his neck. He didn't want to blow his cool. "Well, sure, that's great," he said. "But only if you want. You don't have to."

Dimitri nodded. "We want."

"That's cool," Bondi said, his face breaking into a wide

smile. "What are we waiting for? Let's go."

Melissa grabbed Bondi and Wilf by the hands, and together all of them marched into the building.

Sybil Ambrose-Murgeston

❦ ❦ ❦

Mr. Linus Ambrose
1600 N. Astor Street
Chicago, Il.

Dear Brother,

　Please accept my apologies in advance for wiping the floor with your pathetic self. I would promise to try to go easy on you, but you're such a complete and utter fool that we both know there's no point.

　Enjoy your humiliation, pig.

Sybil

Linus Ambrose

Ms. Sybil Ambrose-Murgeston
1601 N. Astor Street
Chicago, IL

Dear Sister,

Bravo. Your self-delusion is awe-inspiring. I will keep your entertainment value in mind after I inherit everything and KICK YOU OUT ON YOUR PITIFUL MONEY-GRUBBING REAR.

Yours in absolutely no sense of the word,

Linus

Melissa, Bondi, Wilf

Butler looked up and smiled as the kids and drivers filed into the hallway. They'd taken the elevator up to the twenty-fourth floor in silence before walking down the long hallway to the waiting area outside of Colonel McCormick's and Captain Patterson's offices. Melissa was glad she'd printed out a copy of the map. It was a relief to feel like they knew where they were going.

Mr. Smith and a pinch-faced woman loaded down with jewelry were standing impatiently in front of Butler, obviously put out by having to wait.

"Hey there, Mr. Butler, Mr. Smith." Bondi extended his hand to the woman. "Bondi Johnson, ma'am. Good to know you."

Her eyes narrowed, and she looked at his hand like he was offering her a used Kleenex. "Linus," she hissed, *"what is this?"*

A vein in Mr. Smith's forehead started to pulse. "What are you children doing here? This is *not* part of the scholarship competition. I'm afraid you have all forfeited. Now go. *Go!*" He made shooing motions, but no one moved.

Mr. Butler cleared his throat. "As executor of Mr. Ambrose's estate, I should tell you that the children are here at my invitation. They have qualified for this final test and will be competing with you for the inheritance."

"*What?* Competing?" Mr. Smith sputtered. "That's outrageous! They aren't qualified to shine my shoes, let alone compete for my father's fortune. Get rid of them. Get rid of them or you're fired." The vein was pulsing so hard Melissa was afraid it was going to blow.

Butler just smiled. "I'm sorry, but no. The will clearly states that whosoever solves the clues and discerns the location of the final testing shall be eligible to inherit. By sharing your clues, you made them eligible to inherit. And, if I may remind you, your father was my employer, not you."

"Linus, you idiotic fool!" Sybil glared at him with eyes like lasers. "This is just like you." She turned to Butler, her expression suddenly all sweetness and light. "Isn't there any way to correct my brother's error? It was just an unfortunate mistake." She batted her eyes like a cartoon bunny.

"No, there is not. And, interestingly enough," Butler said

calmly, "the will specifically mentions the possibility of a third party joining the competition. It seems that Enoch Ambrose anticipated this turn of events."

"He *what*?" Smith's face had turned a dark purple color. Melissa took a step away from him. She didn't really think his head was going to explode, but she figured she couldn't be too careful. She was wearing a white shirt.

Butler didn't seem to be the least bit concerned by the unusual shade of Linus Ambrose's face. "Enoch Ambrose expected you to bend the rules in just this way, I'm afraid." Mr. Butler gave Linus Ambrose a thin smile. "Now, shall we proceed?"

Sybil turned her back on everyone but Butler. "Yes, Hughes, let's end this farce as quickly as we can."

"Hughes?" Wilf said under his breath.

"William Hughes, Enoch Ambrose's attorney. Linus Ambrose, or 'Smith,' was calling him 'Butler' as a joke," Inez said, making air quotes. "You know, like generic code names, 'Mr. Smith' and his butler. He thought it was a riot."

"Yeah, real funny," Bondi said. These guys were so weird. He wasn't going to feel bad about taking their inheritance at all.

"I'm never going to remember Hughes," Wilf muttered.

"Don't even try. Just think of him like the Sears Tower," Bondi said, patting Wilf on the back. "Nobody calls it the Willis Tower, even if that's its name now."

"Good point," Wilf said, looking happier.

Butler, aka William Hughes, clapped his hands together. "Now! We will interview everyone individually, beginning with Mrs. Ambrose-Murgeston. If you will, Mrs. Murgeston?" Butler ushered her into the open door in front of them.

"That must be the directors' room," Melissa said, nudging Wilf and Bondi. "The conference room in between McCormick's and Patterson's offices."

Wilf nodded. He was glad Melissa had practically memorized that map, because he sure as heck hadn't.

As the doors closed, Linus Ambrose glared at them from the other side of the waiting room. "So done some research, have you? Think you know what's happening here, don't you, missy?" he said to Melissa as he walked slowly toward them. "You all seem to think very highly of yourselves for getting this far. Well, let me set you straight about one thing."

He stopped in front of Bondi and stood so close that Bondi could feel Linus Ambrose's breath on his forehead.

"You think you were selected at random? Or because you were smart? Ha!" He laughed in Bondi's face. "I didn't pick you because you were smart. I picked you because you're losers. Juvenile delinquents. Criminals. Two steps away from jail." Linus Ambrose laughed again, a harsh croaking laugh. "Oh yes, I know all about you. I watched you. All of you." He pointed at Wilf. "Stinking thief. Quick to take advantage, aren't you? Can't pass up little opportunities like dropped tardy slips or unrestricted debit cards. And you . . ." He pointed at Melissa. "Backroom forger. With your black market worksheets, your underhanded business selling homework answers. No better than a common criminal." Melissa had turned white. "Oh yes, I know all about that." Linus Ambrose chuckled and turned back to Bondi. "And you, you're nothing but a con man in the making, Mr. Personality. Working all the angles and manipulating people to get what you want. It's always all about you. You think I didn't see through that?"

Linus Ambrose smirked at them. "I didn't pick you because I thought you were better than anyone else, or 'special.' I picked you because I knew you immoral brats would lie and cheat to solve the problems, and that served my purposes. Well, your criminal scheming may have gotten you here, but it's not going to get you any further. Lowlife scum like you doesn't deserve a penny of Enoch Ambrose's money." He locked eyes with Bondi and then spit on the floor at his feet.

It was like he'd frozen everyone in the room. Wilf opened his mouth, but no sound came out. Even Inez seemed stunned. Bondi slowly looked down at the glob of spit, but he didn't step back. He just silently folded his arms.

Linus Ambrose glared triumphantly at each of them and

then turned his back, strolling over to the door of the directors' room to await his turn.

Bondi and the others were still standing frozen when the door to the directors' room opened. Sybil came out with a superior smile on her face.

Butler stood in the doorway, his hands clasped in front of him. "Mrs. Ambrose-Murgeston has successfully passed this test and will now advance to the last and final level," he announced, frowning slightly at the tension in the room. He looked questioningly at Bondi, but Bondi's expression was blank. Butler turned to Linus Ambrose. "Mr. Ambrose?"

With a triumphant backward glance, Linus Ambrose shoved his way past Butler into the directors' room. Butler nodded to Melissa and the others and then quietly closed the door behind him.

Mrs. Ambrose-Murgeston immediately pulled out her smartphone, stalking over to the corner of the waiting room and ignoring the rest of them completely.

Melissa let out the breath she hadn't even known she was holding. It seemed like the temperature in the room had gone up thirty degrees once Linus Ambrose had left, even taking into account the frosty patch in the corner that was Mrs. Ambrose-Murgeston.

She didn't care what that jerk had to say. She may have forged some worksheets, but that didn't mean a forger was all she was. And no matter what Bondi and Wilf had done, they didn't deserve to be called thieves and con artists. They weren't losers and criminals. And nothing any of them had done made them as bad as Linus Ambrose.

She elbowed Bondi in the ribs. "You okay?"

Bondi nodded.

She toed the floor around the glob of spit, careful not to touch it. "Ew, right? What a loser."

"Don't mind him, he's full of hot air," Frank said quietly, putting his hand on Bondi's shoulder. "What a load of horse hockey."

"He's so mad," Melissa said softly.

"Well, that's Linus for you," Inez said, taking her cigarettes out of her shoulder bag, then reconsidering and tossing them back in unopened. "Grade-A blowhard."

"You are not criminals," Dimitri said, patting Melissa on the shoulder. "He is a sad man."

"He really was mad," Wilf said, looking at Melissa and Bondi. "I mean, really, *really* mad."

"Yeah," Bondi said. "And think how much madder he's going to be when he figures out we gave him the wrong answers." He raised his eyebrows at Wilf and Melissa. Melissa quickly bit her lip, but it was too late. Giggles were already starting to erupt.

"So mad!" She giggled.

"Please excuse, but you did what? Wrong answers?" The corner of Dimitri's mouth twitched, just for a second. But that's all it took to reduce the huddled group into a helpless mass of muffled giggles.

• •

Sybil Ambrose-Murgeston: First test passed. Now waiting with gaggle of giggling idiots. Father's lucky he's dead, or I'd give him a piece of my mind.

Bitsy Worthington Sykes: That dead man wouldn't know what hit him!

Melissa, Wilf, Bondi

They could hear the shouting inside the office, but they still jumped when the door opened and they were hit with the full volume. Even Mrs. Ambrose-Murgeston startled. She recovered quickly, though, and then glared at Bondi like it was his fault.

"YOU LIARS!" Linus Ambrose roared as he barreled into the room, grabbing Bondi by the collar. "You kids think you're so clever. Well, you don't know who you're messing with."

"Take your hands off the child, Mr. Ambrose," Butler said quietly as he appeared in the doorway. "Or believe me, there will be legal repercussions."

"There will be more than legal repercussions if you don't let him go now," Frank said, taking off his jacket and handing it to Inez.

"Repercussions my behind," Ambrose scoffed, but he

dropped Bondi like he was a hot coal. Bondi smoothed his shirtfront and glared back at Linus Ambrose, but his hands were shaking.

Linus leaned toward Wilf, so close that flecks of spit hit Wilf in the face. "You brats think you can cheat me out of my inheritance by being filthy liars?"

Mrs. Ambrose-Murgeston gave a squeal of glee and tucked her phone away in her huge purse. "What's this? You didn't get those questions *wrong*, did you, Linus? They were so *simple*."

"Shut up!" her brother bellowed.

"Mr. Linus Ambrose failed to provide the correct solutions to all the clues," said Butler. "Therefore, he does not advance to the final trial. Mr. Ambrose, if you would please vacate the premises while those still eligible continue?"

Linus Ambrose sputtered like a wick that wouldn't stay lit, his face turning from deep red to dark purple. "You . . . They . . ."

"Children, if you would?" Mr. Butler extended his arm toward the office, inviting the kids inside.

"Absolutely not!" Mr. Ambrose finally found his voice. "Even if it is *within the rules* for these delinquents to participate, they can't *all* go in. You said it yourself—this is an *individual* trial. A bunch of random kids can't all wander in like this is some kind of field trip. It's for *one* heir and *one heir only*."

He glared at Wilf like he was itching to throttle him, too. Wilf inched away from him.

Melissa took a deep breath and stepped forward, so she was practically under Linus Ambrose's nose. "Excuse me, Mr. Ambrose. We are not a bunch of random kids. We come as a set. Sets come in all sizes." She shot a quick smile at Dimitri. "And if I've learned one thing, it's that you can't break up a set." She glared back up at Linus Ambrose, her chin raised defiantly.

Linus Ambrose's hands clenched and unclenched, and then he pushed her out of the way as he headed for the door. "That's it. I'm calling the authorities. You won't get away with this, Hughes!" he yelled at the attorney. "I hope you'll enjoy prison, because that's where you're heading. Mark my words."

Mr. Butler just nodded. "Excellent. Children?" He turned his back on Linus Ambrose as he ushered Melissa, Wilf, and Bondi into the office, ignoring the murderous glare Linus Ambrose shot him as he stormed to the elevator.

To: Chief of Police

From: Sergeant Wilkins

Subject: Illegal activity by Ambrose Family lawyer?

Chief:

We got a call from one Linus Ambrose demanding that we arrest the Ambrose family lawyer for fraud, deceptive practices, grand larceny, corruption, and conspiracy to swindle him out of his inheritance. He says we can catch him in the act right now at the Tribune Tower, 24th floor.

I'm sending officers over, but isn't Linus Ambrose the one who wanted his sister arrested for slander over that newspaper article? Anyway, this could be big.

Sgt. Wilkins

To: Sergeant Wilkins

From: Chief of Police

Subject: RE: Illegal activity by Ambrose Family lawyer?

Linus Ambrose? I've had it with that crackpot and his wild goose chases. Send a couple of officers over and arrest anyone on the premises. We'll sort them out later. A night in jail should teach them a thing or two.

The Chief

Melissa, Bondi, Wilf

"So." Mr. Butler stood in front of the desk and picked up an official-looking leather notebook. "You made it this far. I'm impressed."

"Thanks," Melissa said.

"Yeah, well, we couldn't just let that old guy win, right?" Bondi grinned. "Not once we'd figured out what he was up to."

Whatever the directors' room had been like back in the day, now it was just a basic reception area. There was a desk across from the entrance, and two small couches were positioned along the wall on either side of the room. Beside each couch was a closed door.

"Those are the doors to McCormick's and Patterson's offices, I'm sure of it," Melissa whispered to Wilf. He nodded and rubbed his nose. That mothball/peppermint smell was back and bugging him again, and he couldn't figure out where it was coming from. It wasn't from Butler, he was sure of that.

"Well. Well done," Butler said. He consulted a document in the notebook. "This is an unusual circumstance, because you've already answered these clues once. Do you stand by your previous answers? We won't go through them again if you do, but if you'd like to make a change, this is the time."

"I would," Bondi said quickly. "One of mine before wasn't right. I'd like to change that one."

Butler nodded approvingly. "Certainly. Your previous responses were Buckingham Fountain, the Skydeck Ledge at the Willis Tower, and the staircase at the Rookery. Which of those would you like to change?"

Bondi cleared his throat. "Buckingham Fountain. That's not the right one. It should be the Eli Bates Fountain in Lincoln Park, Storks at Play." He grinned. "Also known as 'Spitty Geese with Fish Huggers.'"

Butler took a silver pen out of his pocket. "Are you all in agreement?" he asked, looking at Wilf and Melissa.

"Yes," Wilf said. Melissa nodded.

"Done." Butler made a notation on his paper and then turned to Melissa. "And you? Any changes to make? You said . . ." He checked the paper again. "Lorado Taft's *Eternal Silence* monument, the frieze known as *Contribution* on the InterContinental Hotel, and Finnigan's Ice Cream Shop and the chick hatchery in the Museum of Science and

Industry. Do you stand by those responses?"

Melissa took a deep breath. She was sure they were right. They had to be. "I do."

Butler made another notation and turned to Wilf. "And you? Do you stand by your responses? They were the *Bowman* and *Spearman* statues at the entrance to Congress Plaza, the Tribune Tower, and the"—he cleared his throat—"Blue Cow Cafe on Michigan Avenue?"

Wilf forced himself not to look at Melissa and Bondi because he knew he'd crack up if he did. "Not the last one. That cafe's in Michigan. The real answer to the last clue is the Mold-A-Rama machine in the barn at Lincoln Park Zoo. It makes a blue cow."

Butler looked like he was trying not to smile. "I see." He made a note on the paper and then put the notebook down on the desk, folding his hands in front of him. He looked at them with a somber expression on his face.

"I should tell you that I didn't expect for you to reach this point, particularly since you were not personally acquainted with Enoch Ambrose. Regardless of the results, you should be proud to have made it this far."

Bondi held his breath. That didn't sound good. They hadn't gotten one wrong, had they? And if they had, which one was it? He didn't want to walk away with a "good try" and a pat on the back. And he hated the idea of that Sybil woman getting the better of him.

Bondi glanced over at Melissa and Wilf. Melissa's fists were clenched at her sides so tightly that her knuckles had turned white, and Wilf was swaying slightly, like he was on the verge of passing out.

Bondi turned back to Butler just in time to see him smile.

Butler extended his hand to Bondi, Melissa, and Wilf in turn. "Congratulations. You have answered all the questions correctly. You will be advancing to the final level. Now, let's tell the others, shall we?"

Wilf was the first one to let loose with a whoop, but it was only a second before the others joined in.

• •

Sybil Ambrose-Murgeston: Si, review my father's will ASAP. There are some irregularities here that are QUITE DISTURBING, namely URCHIN COMPETITORS. If you want to remain my attorney, you need to stop this nonsense. IMMEDIATELY. Unless you want to work for a pack of snot-nosed brats, I expect you to take this seriously. S. A.-M.

Silas Glover: Sybil, how many cocktails have you had today?

Melissa, Wilf, Bondi

"Once again I want to register my extreme disapproval with this entire charade."

Melissa hadn't thought it was possible for Mrs. Ambrose-Murgeston's face to look any more pinched, but boy had she been wrong. Sybil looked like she'd sucked down a whole lemon tree.

"Again, noted," Butler said, a weary tone creeping into his voice. He must have had a list of objections as long as his arm by now.

"Now!" He clapped once. "You have all demonstrated your qualifications by answering the nine clues correctly. But Enoch Ambrose stipulated that there be one final test."

Everyone nodded. Melissa tried to keep herself calm. *One final test.* Did that mean one more question? How bad could it be? But they had no library to go to, no way to do research. If they blew this last part, that was it.

"As you know, this was once the directors' room of the Tribune Company, run by Colonel Robert McCormick and Captain Joseph Patterson. These were their offices." He indicated the doors to his sides. "Your final challenge is this: One of these doors leads to the entire Ambrose fortune. The other leads to nothing at all. Choose the door that you prefer, and everything you find within will be yours. But choose wisely. Which will it be? The door to my left, or the door to my right? You will have five minutes to make your decision."

"What if we pick the same one as her?" Wilf pointed at Sybil.

"We will handle that contingency should it arise," Butler said. "And remember, one points you forward, one takes you back, and one is a trick." He looked at his watch. "Your five minutes start now."

"I wish he hadn't said that points-you-forward-takes-you-back part," Wilf said quietly. "I hate that part."

"Only because you don't know what it means," Melissa said.

"Exactly," Wilf said.

Sybil Ambrose-Murgeston smiled to herself and made a big show of sitting down on one of the soft couches and examining her nails. Then she yawned like a bored, pampered cat in a Fancy Feast commercial. She obviously didn't need the five minutes to make her decision.

"So this is it, huh?" Bondi said softly. "It comes down to this. So the one on the left, that's McCormick's office?"

Melissa nodded. She didn't need the map of the office building anymore, she'd stared at it so long. She even remembered where Miss Higgins had sat, and she didn't even know who the heck Miss Higgins was.

"So which one? McCormick or Patterson? I vote McCormick," Bondi whispered, eyeing Sybil warily.

"McCormick," Wilf agreed. "Definitely."

Melissa nodded. "McCormick."

"Well, that was easy." Bondi smiled. "Man, I hope we're right."

Wilf shrugged. "It has to be him, right? I mean, that's what my clue said, the co-editor in charge of the moon, right? And he's the one everyone remembers."

Melissa frowned. Something didn't seem right with that, but she wasn't sure what. "That's true, but . . ." she said hesitantly.

"And McCormick's the one Ambrose was always pranking," Bondi said. "So, ready?"

Wilf nodded. Melissa was staring at the floor. Wilf nudged her. "Ready?"

"Oh, yeah. Right," Melissa said finally.

Bondi looked down at her, his expression serious. "Hey. Right? Or have you thought of something? There's still time."

Melissa bit her lip but nodded. "No, right. I mean, that must be it. It's just that—"

The sound of Butler clapping drowned out Melissa's voice. Bondi cocked his head to the side, but Melissa just shrugged and shook her head.

"All right! Now, you have a choice to make," Mr. Butler said. "And remember, everything you know, everything you've done up to this point should lead you to the right answer."

Butler turned to Mrs. Ambrose-Murgeston. "As it has no bearing upon the results, we will begin with the children." She rolled her eyes but waved her hand languidly, as if she were a queen granting his request.

"Now," Butler continued. "Which of you will be answering for the team?" He looked at Bondi, but Bondi shook his head.

He nudged Melissa in the side. "It should be you. Go with your gut. We trust you."

Butler turned to Melissa. "Miss Burris, please speak for your team. Which of the two rooms do you select?"

Melissa swallowed hard. Bondi and Wilf were right. It had to be McCormick.

"We select the room . . ." she said, her voice squeaking. She cleared her throat and started again. She opened her mouth to say McCormick. She meant to say McCormick. "We select the room . . ." And suddenly all the pieces fell into place.

She shot an apologetic look at Wilf and Bondi. "We select the room on the right. Captain Patterson's office." Melissa's eyes widened at what she'd heard herself say.

Bondi gave a low whistle.

Wilf stared down at the floor. "Wow," he muttered.

Melissa looked up at Butler, hoping to see approval on his face, but he had already turned to Sybil. "And you, Mrs. Ambrose-Murgeston?"

"The room on the left, of course. Colonel McCormick's office. *Obviously.*" She smirked at Melissa and stood up, smoothing her skirt.

"Very good. Your choices have been made." Butler was expressionless as he opened a drawer in the desk and took something out.

He handed a skeleton key to Melissa and another almost identical key to Sybil. Then he leaned back against the desk, his arms folded. "May you enjoy your rewards."

"Patterson? *Patterson?* What the heck, Melissa?" Wilf hissed as they headed to Captain Patterson's office door.

"You thought of something, didn't you? I knew it!" Bondi said. "Please tell me you thought of something."

"How could she think of something? It was McCormick! His daughter knows it! The clue said it—*co-editor in charge of the moon.*"

"No!" Melissa stopped. "The clue said *beloved* co-editor in charge of the moon. And McCormick *wasn't* beloved by Ambrose. He would *never* call him that. That clue must've been about Patterson. McCormick, he was just the trick! Plus, Patterson's office is on the north side of the building. McCormick's is on the south."

"So?" Wilf said, sniffing.

"Patterson's office is the one that faces the *Contribution* frieze on the InterContinental Hotel. Not McCormick's office. And remember? One points you forward, one takes you back, and one is a trick? The frieze takes you forward toward the prize. It's the one showing the *presentation of riches*. This *has* to be it!"

"Or it's the trick," Wilf muttered.

"It was always a crapshoot, anyway. Let's see what's inside," Bondi said, pointing at the key in Melissa's hand.

She turned it over once and then handed it to Wilf. "You do it," she said. "I hope I didn't mess this whole thing up for you."

Wilf took the key and weighed it in his hand. Then he looked up at Melissa and smiled. "Well, it's not like we'll be any worse off if we're wrong, right? And this was a lot of fun, hanging out with you guys. Here goes nothing!" He sniffed again. "Ugh, sorry. Man, where is that smell coming from?" he said apologetically. It was driving him crazy.

"Forget the smell. Just open it," Bondi said.

They opened the door to Captain Patterson's office just as Mrs. Ambrose-Murgeston opened the door on the other side of the room. Hearts racing, they hurried inside. Then they stopped short.

The room was empty.

. . . .

Ways to Cheer Yourself Up When You Win the Contents of an Empty Room

by Bondi Johnson, Wilf Samson, and Melissa Burris

1. Hey, materialism stinks, right? Who needs possessions? —Bondi
2. AT LEAST IT'S NOT UGLY STUFF YOU HAVE TO SELL. —WILF
3. Don't have much spare room in the house, anyway. —Bondi
4. How would we have gotten all those riches home? Very impractical. —Melissa

. . . .

"Well, I wasn't thinking it would be empty," Melissa said, her voice thick. The walls of the room were paneled in dark

343

wood and broken up on the north and west by large, impressive windows.

"Guess we should've picked the other room," Wilf shrugged, kicking the floor.

"Well—" Bondi started. But before he'd gotten more than one word out, the sound of Mrs. Ambrose-Murgeston's screams filled the room. They weren't happy screams.

"Well, maybe not," Bondi said, perking up. "She doesn't sound too pleased over there. Maybe there's still a chance?"

"Maybe." Wilf snickered. "Boy, she's ticked."

"Hey, guys, see?" Melissa was leaning on the ledge of the north-facing window. "See there, you *can* see the *Contribution* frieze from here! I knew I was right!"

"That does seem like a good sign," Bondi said, craning his neck to look up at the wood paneling on the east wall. "But the room's still empty. You were right about one thing, though—these panels are amazing. If I didn't know there was a door in this wall, I'd never guess."

"Yeah, but it was McCormick who used to play that trick on his visitors, not Patterson," Wilf said, rubbing his nose.

"But they both could have. . . ." Bondi looked around thoughtfully. "The offices are mirror images of each other, right? If McCormick's office is empty, too, there's got to be something we're missing."

"Got to be," Wilf said, digging in his pocket for a Kleenex. "Sorry, that peppermint smell is killing me."

"It's in here, too?" Melissa said.

"Stronger than ever." Wilf blew his nose.

"Mirror images," Bondi repeated, examining the panel closest to him. He jimmied the edge, and the panel swung open to reveal a closet.

"Right. Oh man, that's a hidden closet!" Melissa rushed over to inspect it.

"Yeah. An *empty* closet," Wilf pointed out.

"Yeah, but there's a secret stairway in McCormick's office, right?" Bondi's eyes gleamed.

"Right. So there's one in here, too!" Melissa slammed the closet door shut and rushed over to the west wall. "It should be over here somewhere . . ." she said, running her hands up and down the paneling.

"That's so perfect—he must've hidden the inheritance in the secret stairway!" Wilf and Bondi quickly high-fived each other before rushing over to join in the hunt.

Mrs. Ambrose-Murgeston was still screaming bloody murder in the other office, which seemed like a good sign. It was mostly cursing, it sounded like, with some abuse being thrown at her father, at Butler (or Hughes, as she called him), and at the world in general thrown in for good measure.

Melissa reached the corner where the wall turned to

create a window nook. She ran her hands up the edge and then caught her breath. Her finger had just caught on something.

"Guys, I think I—"

Bondi cut Melissa off with a hiss. "*Shh*—listen!" They froze, listening to the screams from the other office. Their tone had changed.

Mrs. Ambrose-Murgeston was no longer ranting about how Butler was going to jail. Other voices had joined hers, and one was shouting louder than the rest. A voice Bondi and Melissa and Wilf all recognized. Mr. Linus Ambrose's voice.

"It's Smith! He's back!" Bondi didn't move a muscle.

Wilf crept quietly over to the partially open door and peeked through. "I think those are cops," he whispered, his eyes wide. "He really brought the cops."

Bondi felt panic rising in his chest. "Oh man. We only have a minute before they come in here, too," he whispered. "Wilf, the door!"

Wilf nodded, then slowly and silently nudged the office door shut with his foot. They waited, afraid to move, for a long thirty seconds. Melissa knew. She'd counted.

Melissa reached back up and examined the piece of the wall that had caught her finger. A small knob was embedded in the wood. A strangled sob-laugh rose in her throat. "Guys, I found it!"

She grabbed the knob and pulled it gently. The entire section of panel swung open, revealing a shallow opening in the wall and a narrow stairway leading up into darkness.

"The secret stairway," Bondi breathed.

"You can't arrest me! It's those *brats* you should be arresting!" Sybil's voice was harsh and grating. "They're in there!"

"Quick!" Bondi ducked into the stairway, dragging Wilf and Melissa behind him. They'd barely gotten the door shut when they heard footsteps coming into the room.

"So this is the secret stairway, huh?" Wilf whispered. He couldn't see anything, but he could hear Bondi and Melissa breathing hard. "Guess we know where the peppermint smell was coming from."

Melissa sniffed. She could smell it now, too. "Yeah, I see what you mean. Bondi, we should go up. We can't go back out now, not with the cops there." If they didn't know about the secret stairway, she wasn't about to clue them in. And there was no way she was getting arrested. Mrs. Orlin would never shut up about it if she did.

"Right," Bondi whispered. "My keychain has a light . . . hold on."

Melissa could hear Bondi fiddling with something, and then a dim light illuminated his face. Or part of it. It was a tiny beam of light.

"Okay, let's go up." Bondi started slowly climbing the

stairs, the pinprick of light leading the way. Melissa and Wilf climbed after him.

"I bet the treasure's at the top," Wilf said quietly, trying not to breathe too loudly. Bondi was breathing hard enough for both of them. He hoped he was okay.

"Bondi, you all right?" Wilf finally said. "If you need to take a break, we can."

Bondi half turned to face him. "What? Why would I?"

"You sound pretty bad, buddy." Wilf hated to say it flat out like that, but somebody had to.

"Your breathing," Melissa said softly.

Bondi stopped short. "I thought that was you."

Wilf froze. "It's not."

"It's not me, either."

The three of them stared at each other in the yellowy light from Bondi's keychain, listening to the low, raspy breathing filling the secret stairway.

Eyes wide, Bondi shone the weak light up step after step until it reached the dark space at the top.

"SURPRISE!"

The raspy voice made Bondi and Melissa jump so violently that they almost toppled backwards onto Wilf. There, illuminated in the weak light from Bondi's keychain, a face was leering down at them.

The face of Enoch Ambrose.

How to Choose Between the Police and a Dead Guy

by Melissa Burris, Wilf Samson,
and Bondi Johnson

1. There is no choice. Just die right where you're standing. —Melissa
2. YEAH, SERIOUSLY. (NO REALLY, IF YOU HAVE TO CHOOSE, GO WITH THE DEAD GUY. A FEW WELL- PLACED KICKS SHOULD TAKE HIM OUT, RIGHT?) —WILF
3. Is there a third option? —Bondi
4. KICKS, RIGHT? (RIGHT?) —WILF

"Boy, am I glad to see you!"

"Enoch Ambrose? But . . . you're dead?" Melissa stammered, trying really hard not to barf.

Enoch Ambrose was perched at the top of the stairs like some kind of ancient spider, grinning like he'd just won the lottery.

"Says who? Can't trust anything you read in the papers these days." Ambrose stretched his legs and scuttled down a few steps until he was right next to them.

"So you're *not* dead?" Wilf really didn't want to try to fight a dead guy. He thought he could probably take him no problem, but he didn't want to find out.

"Do I look dead?" Enoch Ambrose mugged like he was posing for a picture.

"No," Wilf admitted. "And you don't smell dead. That peppermint smell is you, isn't it?"

Enoch Ambrose sniffed his shirt. "I suppose so."

"And I smelled that on the first day," Wilf said accusingly. "You've been in on this the whole time!"

Enoch Ambrose shrugged. "Well, what's the point of planning a big inheritance scheme if you aren't around to enjoy it? You bet I was there the whole time, and those greedy kids of mine never suspected! I knew that boy Linus would try to cheat and ruin my fun." He leaned in conspiratorially. "So what's going on? Sybil picked McCormick's office?"

Melissa nodded. "She seemed pretty sure of herself."

Enoch gave a wheezy chuckle. "She always was starstruck by that blowhard. If she understood me at all, she'd know that McCormick stuff was all a trick." He leaned forward again, grinning. "Well, I showed her. Know what was hidden in McCormick's hidden stairway? Big bucket of stinky dead fish, that's what. Nothing Sybil hates more!"

"Oh man, that's harsh," Wilf said. He was starting to like this guy.

"Yep, a couple of cold fish, that's what my kids turned out to be. Boy was I glad when Willie told me about you kids!"

"Willie?" Melissa said weakly.

"Willie Hughes, my lawyer. Butler, he's been calling himself, for Linus's scam. He's been a real peach, sneaking me around so I can keep tabs on Linus and his schemes. They never suspected a thing, not when I was right under their noses. But it worked out, didn't it? Now let me guess, did Linus call the cops?"

"Yeah," Wilf said.

"And they're down there now?"

"I think so," Melissa said. "It sounded like they were arresting people."

"Oh, we can't miss that. Besides, it's time we got you introduced. I want the world to meet my three smart kids, the new Ambrose heirs!"

**INHERITANCE SHOCKER!
ENOCH AMBROSE ALIVE!**
Psychic claims to have seen all

**ECCENTRIC BILLIONAIRE NAMES
JUVENILE DELINQUENTS AS HEIRS**

Ambrose children's lawsuit thrown
out of court

DEATH HOAX SHOCKER!!
Ambrose billionaire faked his own
death. Could others be next? We
discover Elvis, Tupac, and Gandhi
LIVING IN DAYTONA BEACH.

I KNEW PRETEEN CON ARTIST
*One guidance counselor opens up about her
disturbing experiences with preteen con artist
turned Ambrose heir*

Melissa, Wilf, Bondi

"Wow, that last article really isn't fair," Melissa said, throwing the newspaper on the table. "Mrs. Orlin is having a hard time letting this go. Thank goodness Ambrose fixed it so me and Tanisha can go to Noyes Central with you and Bondi."

"Yeah, I was psyched that Ambrose could get me out of Sutherland. Bondi's friends seem cool, too," Wilf said absentmindedly as he pointed to a different headline. "Is this stuff true? About Elvis?"

Melissa rolled her eyes. "What do you think? Did we really . . . ?" She picked up another paper and read out loud: ". . . creep like a cancer into Linus Ambrose's happy home, conning the aged bachelor with false displays of filial affection, all the while secretly plotting to steal his fortune?"

"Well, no," Wilf said. "I guess not."

"You should see the stuff they're saying online. It's even

worse." Melissa snorted. One of the first things Enoch Ambrose had done (after straightening things out with the police) was replace their crappy loaner phones and get them all set up with what he called "life accoutrement"—up-to-date smartphones, laptops to use for schoolwork, and weekly allowances so that Melissa could leave the world of black market worksheets behind. She didn't miss it. (Tyler Blake sure did, though.)

Enoch Ambrose hobbled over to the table, weighed down with a heavy tray from the Lincoln Park Zoo snack bar. "Who wants a hot dog? Wilf, I know you do."

Wilf turned pale. "Not for me, thanks."

Enoch Ambrose chuckled. "That was a hoot to hear about, I have to tell you. Hot dog taste test competition! What an idea. You're a chip off the old block. You all are."

He grabbed a fry and chomped down on it.

"What do you mean?" Melissa said, taking Wilf's rejected hot dog. "Linus said we were criminals. He called us thieves and con artists and liars."

Ambrose chortled, dribbling ketchup on the table. "Linus is an idiot. Never had time for my tomfoolery, as he called it. Now this one"—he ruffled Wilf's hair—"he has my sense of adventure and fun; that was clear from the get-go. That Bondi, he's a hard worker and a people person. He's going places. And Melissa, you're my little entrepreneur. You know what Linus is? A drip, that's what. Sybil, too. Two world-class drips," he finished, waving the french fry in the air for emphasis. "Where is that Bondi, anyway?"

Melissa pointed in the direction of the zoo barn. "Here he comes."

"Guys, check it out." Bondi plunked something round and orange down in the middle of the table.

Melissa poked it with a finger. "What is that?" It looked like a little orange tennis ball with legs.

"It's a wax pig from the Mold-A-Rama machine," Bondi said.

"Plastic," Wilf said, his mouth full of fries.

"It's a *plastic* pig from the Mold-A-Rama machine," Bondi said, shooting Wilf a nasty look.

"What?" Melissa looked shocked. "No more blue cows?"

"I guess not," Bondi said. "Good thing we figured out that clue when we did. Hey, way to go, picking a clue that changes, Gramps." He plopped down onto the bench next to Enoch Ambrose.

"Well, how was I supposed to know they'd change the animal?" Ambrose grumbled, trying to keep from smiling. He was looking really good for a formerly dead guy. Much better than he'd looked at the end of "Enoch Ambrose: The Later Years."

"Melissa!"

She looked up to see her grandmother trotting over from the direction of the seal pool. Gran's expression was nonchalant, but Melissa noticed her hair was freshly done and she was wearing lipstick.

"Why, Mr. Ambrose, how lovely to meet you. Melissa has told me so much about you." Gran coolly extended her hand, like she was meeting one of Melissa's teachers or something. She definitely wasn't acting like someone who owned the complete set of the *Ambrose Chronicles*, Volumes 1–6, from Time-Life Books.

"It's a pleasure, madam." Enoch Ambrose wiped his mouth on a napkin. Then he stood, took Gran's hand, and kissed it.

Gran blushed and withdrew her hand with obvious effort, turning her attention back to Melissa. "Now, Melissa, I'll be back in about an hour. Mrs. Lewis wants me to meet her new friend. Katya or Katrinka or something, I can't remember. You'll keep an eye on Liam?"

Melissa nodded. "He's with Dimitri and Inez and Frank. They wanted to check out the antelopes." Melissa was glad to see her grandmother going out with her friends, even when it wasn't McDonald's day. Heck, it was good to be able to hang out with her own friends without having to worry so much now. Her new friends. Melissa looked around the table and smiled.

"That sounds fine. I'll be back soon. Good-bye, Mr. Ambrose. It was an honor. " She patted her hair and then turned and walked away, only glancing back two or three times.

Enoch Ambrose watched her go. "And who was that vision of loveliness?"

"That was my grandmother," Melissa said, putting the french fry down. She had a feeling she was about to lose her appetite.

"*Rowr.*" Enoch Ambrose's eyes glittered.

Bondi blinked. "Did he just say '*rowr*'?"

Melissa nodded. "He did. *Rowr.*" She made a cat claw motion with her hand.

Bondi put down his burger. "I think I'm going to be sick."

To: Enoch Ambrose

From: William Hughes

Subject: Tying up loose ends

Might I say you have excellent taste in heirs? Also, are there any changes that you would like made with your arrangements?

To: William Hughes

From: Enoch Ambrose

Subject: RE: Tying up loose ends

First things first, I sure do. Those kids are good as gold.

Second, give those drivers raises. And bonuses for all of them. The kids are crazy about them. They're worth every penny.

Third, give Linus and Sybil each a small trust, and inform them that they must make their own way in the world from now on. And tell them that if they whine, they get nothing.

Finally, the kids and I went to the zoo the other day, and we have a serious problem that we need to address AT ONCE.

To: Enoch Ambrose
From: William Hughes
Subject: RE: Tying up loose ends

Agreed. It will be taken care of immediately.

To: William Hughes
From: The Lawson Atwater Center, Antarctica
Subject: Happy to help

Sir,
We have received your request, and we can certainly help you out. How many penguins do you think you'll need?

AUTHOR'S NOTE

Colonel Robert McCormick and his cousin Captain Joseph Patterson were real people. They were co-editors of the *Chicago Tribune* from 1914–1926 and worked in identical offices on the twenty-fourth floor of the Tribune Tower. The floor plan on page 309 shows the actual layout of the twenty-fourth floor, complete with McCormick's and Patterson's secret stairways.

When I visited the Tribune Tower, those two offices were unoccupied and used for special events, and the hidden stairways were being used for storage purposes. And in 2016, the Tribune Tower was sold, ending its long historic association with the *Chicago Tribune*. At this point, the future of the Tribune Tower is still very much an open question.

All of the locations in the book are real places that you can visit, although the hours of operation and the animals you can create in the Mold-A-Rama machines may vary depending on the time of year. (The schools are the exception—they're not real schools, so you can't visit those. But really, would you want to?)

Enoch Ambrose and his children are, unfortunately (or not, depending on who you're talking about), fictitious.

At the time this book was written, there were no penguins at the Lincoln Park Zoo. Their exhibit had been shut down in 2011. However, after this book was completed, the zoo announced that it would be bringing penguins back.

Coincidence? (Okay, probably.)

Eli Bates Fountain in Lincoln Park, *Storks at Play*
(aka "Spitty Geese with Fish Huggers")

Acknowledgments

This book would not exist without the hard work of so many talented people, so I want to give special thanks to Kate Schafer Testerman, Stephanie Owens Lurie, Gilbert Ford, and everyone at Disney Hyperion. You guys are rock stars.

Thanks also to:

President Obama, whose visit to Chicago kept me stuck in traffic long enough to come up with the idea for *The Ambrose Deception*.

My cabdriver that day, whose attempt to avoid the traffic jams took me past landmarks (like the *Bowman* and *Spearman* statues) that ultimately ended up in the book.

Amy Dickinson, Jan Guszynski, Gerri Cobb, and John Dewey, for answering my questions and making it possible for me to see Colonel McCormick's and Captain Patterson's offices, even though a movie shoot was going on.

The producers of *Dhoom 3*, for waiting until I'd gotten to see the secret stairways before kicking me off their movie set.

Everyone at *Wait Wait . . . Don't Tell Me!*, for listening to me obsess about Mold-A-Rama machines and the brightness of Divvy bike headlights. And to my SCBWI friends for the advice and moral support.

Katherine Solomonson, for her book, *The Chicago Tribune Tower Competition: Skyscraper Design and Cultural Change in the 1920s*. Thanks also to the incredibly helpful people at Lincoln Park Zoo and Graceland Cemetery.

And finally to my family, for reading a million drafts and putting up with my more-than-occasional author anxiety.